THE GOLDEN SWAN

Nancy Springer

A TIMESCAPE BOOK
PUBLISHED BY POCKET BOOKS NEW YORK

Another *Original* publication of TIMESCAPE BOOKS

A Timescape Book published by
POCKET BOOKS, a Simon & Schuster division of
GULF & WESTERN CORPORATION
1230 Avenue of the Americas, New York, N.Y. 10020

Copyright © 1983 by Nancy Springer

ISBN: 0-671-45253-3

First Pocket Books printing May, 1983

10 9 8 7 6 5 4 3 2 1

Printed in the U.S.A.

The loom, and on the loom
The vatic colors woven,
The prophecies within the web.

The lake, and in the lake
The mirroring reflection,
The shadowshining face of fate.

The grove, and in the grove
The riddle of the goddess,
The dwelling of the guessing god.

Prologue

In her secluded valley in the midlands of Isle lived Ylim, the weaving seeress, and thither rode young King Trevyn with Dair, his small son. Dair was a wolf. Leggy, half grown, he bounded along by the horse, his paws huge and playful, his slate gray fur unruly. Sometimes Trevyn smiled and slapped the saddle, and the yearling wolf would leap up to ride with him for a while. Dair was a wolf because his mother had been one at the time of his birth. She had since taken back her human form and returned across the sea to Tokar, Trevyn surmised. He was a Very King and a sorcerer in the truest sense; the kiss of the goddess was on him. But he did not know what to do for Dair. Destiny is a personal matter.

The young wolf entered the cottage at his heels and sat courteously by his side. *"Laifrita thae, Ilderweyn,"* said Trevyn to Ylim. "Sweet peace to thee, Grandmother." It was the Old Language, the language of the Beginning, which only a special few still remembered. She was not his grandmother in fact, though she might have been grandmother of earth and moon.

"Laifrita thae, Alberic." She called Trevyn by his elfin name. *"Laifrita thae, Dair, how are you?"*

Quite well, Grandmother, thank you. His voice was a murmur or a growl. Only these special ones could understand him, they who conversed with the animals as all men once had.

"Is it good, being a wolf?"

It is very good. The smells, and the air in my nostrils, the chase and the warm meat—He stopped with a side-long look at Trevyn, afraid of being laughed at. He had

7

only recently killed his first rabbit; more often he ate at the king's table and slept by the king's bed. But both Ylim and Trevyn listened to him soberly.

"He is quite content," Trevyn said, "and I am glad of it. But I wish I knew what is to become of him, Grandmother."

"Look your fill," she said.

Dair looked as well. Most folk when they looked on the work of that loom saw nothing. Some who saw could not remember afterward. But Dair saw and remembered well enough. Light, it was all light, not cloth; mauve and lavender light. Then a striking feral face appeared. Broad forehead, brows that darkly met, nostrils that pulsed, wideset amethyst eyes that moved to meet his—that *were* his. A human face, but unmistakably his connate face, his own.

"A regal face," Trevyn said in a hushed voice. Even as he spoke the face shifted form, became a flower such as no one had ever seen before, a blossom made of fire and dew. It blazed and flamed; then as they blinked it dwindled and vanished into the orchid light. The web on the loom went gridelin gray—

Now what? Dair wondered, puzzled. *Shadowy water—*

It was a lake, the most still and waiting of lakes, its smooth surface glinting iron gray, willows on its verge hanging moss gray in breathless, sunless air. On the dim water a swan floated with scarcely a ripple.

"Strange water," said Trevyn.

The swan was black, its image in the water, white. It had been hurt or crippled somehow, for one wing hung limp. But in a moment the wing had healed and it was flying, and it had turned white, pure shining white. It circled and flew nearer, near—the water drew nearer as well. But it was no longer the still lake water. It was purple tinged and restless. The swan vanished or became the whitecaps of that sea.

Ocean, Dair murmured.

A vast expanse. He knew that cold, swelling, limitless expanse that surrounded Isle—and amidst all that vastness a speck, a floating cockleshell, a mere bauble of a boat, a coracle—and in it a solitary—

Who is that?

"Watch," said Ylim.

Closer, always closer. They could see the face now. A youth with russet hair, freckles on the high cheekbones, fine, rugged features and a keen, seeking look about his clear brown eyes. One hand was on a steering oar. The other hung useless from a shriveled arm and shoulder— Dair felt his heart turn over. Without knowing he had moved he found himself standing with his front paws on the frame of the loom, and in a blink the vision vanished. He faced featureless cloth.

"Who was it?" Ylim asked.

I—don't know. But already he felt the mystic bond.

"You will know him well someday," Ylim said.

"Perhaps you will voyage with him out on that sea," Trevyn mused. Dair turned to him in sharp distress.

But Father, I never want to leave you.

Trevyn smiled, a warm, companionable smile. "It is in the nature of human young to leave their parents," he said.

But I am a wolf. And it is in the nature of wolves to be loyal.

"You are more than wolf or human either," said Ylim. "Whose was the face, the first one?"

Mine. He did not hesitate to claim it. She nodded.

"And it is the face of an immortal. You are the son of Maeve the Moon Mother and Trevyn Elfborn, he who brought the magic back from Elwestrand to Isle. That was a turning of the great tide, a greater marvel than you can well imagine, and you were born of that magic." She eyed him sternly. "Dair, the web does not show its wonders for just anyone, you know. Fate may well take you away from your father and Isle."

Dair only whimpered.

"He is very young," Trevyn excused him. "That one on the boat—do you think he is part of Dair's destiny?"

"He and the swan, somehow. Ay."

"Who is he? Where does he come from?"

"How can I know?" Ylim grumbled. "I don't direct my weaving, Alberic, any more than you direct your dreams." For Trevyn's dreams were the font of the magic of Isle.

"And the flower, the lake—"

"I don't know."

"And how Dair's human form is to come to him—"

Ylim merely smiled.

"Answer me just this one question, Ylim," Trevyn requested. "The large question. What part have you seen in the pattern for Dair?"

She hesitated. "Dair," she said to the young wolf at

9

last, "this is not binding. The pattern is ever changing. You may yet change it yourself."

I understand, Dair said.

"The pattern then is this: that you shall continue what your father has begun. That you shall carry magic onward to the mainland."

Fern flower, fire flower,
Burn, burn when the great tide turns.
Fern flower, show your power.
The Swan Lord will be there to see,
To grasp the stem that burns
And speak with thee,
   learn melody,
    and sing with wind and tree.

Fern flower, fire flower,
Bloom, bloom when the true time comes.
Fern flower, share your power.
The wandering wolf will bear your seed
And take you as his doom,
For all men free
   your harmony.
The tide has turned indeed.

book one
DAIR

Chapter One

I am Dair. I am spirit, speaking to you mind to mind, for I know no other way to speak the languages of men. As a man I was a mute because I was born a wolf and stayed so until I was grown—until the day I found Frain.

I had dreamed of him ever since I had seen him on Ylim's loom. It is hard to explain how much he meant to me, this bond brother I had never met. There was something in me that could not forget him. Perhaps it was the wolfwit, which forms attachments for life. Or perhaps it was my father's ardent Laueroc blood. His forebears, the Sun Kings, had been blood brothers and legendary friends, and then there had been his own bond with the god in the grove—or perhaps it was something of the elf in him that would not let me lose sight of the Swan Lord who was coming. Whatever moved me, hardly a day went by that I did not think of the russet-haired youth as I had seen him, afloat on the lonely sea, his destiny somehow mixed in with mine. I wondered and longed for him all that year. I grew restless and took to roaming the downs even as far as the Westwood.

"Wanderlust," Trevyn grumbled. "Dair, you young fur-brained fool, would you please be careful? I worry about you when you are out alone." There was still much hard feeling against wolves in Isle. It had been only a few years since the war when evil sorcery had turned them to a horror, and even Trevyn's good magic could not erase that memory.

No one can come near me, I bragged. *I go like a shadow on the wind.* I was well grown, strong and swift as mountain water.

"Indeed." Trevyn sat back studying me, and for some reason he sighed. He had a human child now, an infant, his legal heir, but always he greeted me with warmth and joy. Truly, I had not meant to go so far from him. But fate had its finger on me. My second snowy winter came and my unrest deepened as the snow.

Sometime after the solstice of that winter I left. The dream of the bond brother was on me, I felt the focus of his coming in the east, and I ran that way to meet him.

I journeyed far faster than any horse. I needed only a coney caught in the snow or a mouse or two and then I was off, padding, night and day, slipping like a slate blue shadow across Isle. For some weeks I went straight as an arrow, straight as arrowflight in silence, until I came to the eastern shore. There on the shingle beach I sat, trying to whiff the smell of destiny in the wind that came across the salt water. Finally I lay down, curling my warm tail over my nose. I lay there for three days.

I was stubbornly waiting. I would not move to hunt for food even though deer ran by within a hundred feet. Snow fell and covered me. Then the clouds drew away and a cold, cold night came. Every star showed, and all the stardark between, and all the warmth of earth seemed to have vanished into that void. There was a looming feeling in the night or in me. I got up and stretched myself for a moment and looked out over the dim ocean, feeling myself tiny in the sight of those twin eyes, sea and sky. There was a steady lapping sound out on the far water that I could not identify. Even my nose told me nothing. All night I sat and watched the dark water and saw nothing. I remembered such dark water from an old woman's loom.

In the morning some instinct sent me northward a little way, and there he lay, naked, the salt spray turning to white rime ice on him.

Frain. The Swan Lord. I did not yet know him by those names, but I knew how important he was to me, and for a horrible moment I thought he was dead. He was lying on the hard, seawashed sand below the high tide ledge, his red hair snarled like wrack, his face far too pale—as pale as sand and snow. But he still breathed, I saw. I lay down right on top of him, trying to warm him with my thick fur, and at that touch a pang of yearning made me howl aloud and the change came on me all in a moment.

It was not of my doing or deciding. These things are often awkward—I might have been of more use to him as a wolf. But it came on me willy-nilly, amid a welter of emotions, compassion—it is the most human of emotions—and longing—I wanted his smile, I had come all this way to meet him, to be his friend, his human friend, it seemed. . . . Cold is what I remember first. The day was as bitterly cold as the night had been. Cold air and cold snow and sand—my fur was gone. I was practically hairless. How humans were to be pitied, to be always so naked beneath their clothes, so cold! I pitied myself heartily. My limbs shot out, long, and my heart pounded within great broad ribs. My muzzle disappeared. My vision blurred for a moment, then righted itself, and hands waved foolishly in front of my face. I was terrified, startled beyond telling. I sprang up to run off. But my limbs would no longer serve me wolf fashion, and I fell over on my side, thrashing. One foot struck Frain, and he groaned.

I had hurt him. I wanted to howl again.

Instead I quieted myself, gathered my wits a moment. Then I struggled up enough to balance on one front paw—hand. I used the other to tug and shake at him. His only reaction was to swallow. I tugged harder, then managed to sit on my haunches and get both hands free. I grasped him under the shoulders, pushed with my feet and sprawled over backwards, pulling him a little farther from the sea. I wanted to get him out of reach of the tide, though it meant dragging him into the snow. But I was barely able to wriggle out from under him. A few more such efforts and I was exhausted.

I was very weak. I had not eaten in too long a time for a human, it seemed. And I was cold, shivering, a horrible, strange sensation to me. I felt terribly afraid. I would freeze, we would both freeze, unless I found us help—

I tried to rise on my long hind legs, to walk man fashion. I fell. Again I tried, and again I fell, and again and again. I gave in and tried to go on four legs, but all my speed and grace and strength had left me; I could go no better than a snail. The nearest dwelling might be miles. . . . Despair washed over me like an incoming tide, and I bowed my head to the ground. This bond brother I had found, I was failing him in every way. I could not carry him to shelter, and I had no longer even any fur to warm him. I had thought that once we were together all things would come to rights, but we were naked, helpless, no

16

better than mewling babes. I whimpered like the babe in its basket back at Laueroc. Then I whined dismally. Finally I raised my head and gave forth with a longdrawn, loud and woebegone howl.

And from the distance an answering shout came.

Trevyn. I should have known he would be anxious, that he would be searching for me, babe or no babe—I should have known. Dear Trevyn. I rose to my knees so that he could see me. He came thundering toward me over the wealds at the head of a half dozen men, looking angry and frightened both at once. When he saw me the look changed to one of astonishment. He brought his horse right up to me, pulling it to a plunging halt.

"Dair?" he cried out. "Dair!"

Thrown off balance, I fell over again. Hot liquid had started down my face at the sight of him. Tears. I would have known what it was if I had thought, but I was appalled by the feeling and by the spasms that had hold of me, the sobs. Trevyn knelt beside me and put his arms around me, folded me into the shelter of his cloak and of his embrace, trying to comfort me.

"Dair," he whispered, "Dair, my son," and he rocked me gently in his arms. "It will be better soon, truly it will."

How did he know what I was feeling, the fear, the pain? But of course he would. He was wise. With some small surprise I saw that he was weeping too. Somehow his tears strengthened me. I straightened, looking for the youth I had found by the sea. The men had already brought him up beside us.

"It is *he*," Trevyn breathed. "The one—"

We saw in Ylim's web. I know.

Trevyn reached over and felt at him, checking his breathing and pulse.

"He's more than half dead," one of the men said.

"Cover him warmly and get him in all haste to Nemeton. There are doctors there." Trevyn fastened his cloak around me and stood up, helping me up as well, supporting me.

"You are as tall as I," he marveled.

It was true. We were two youths. He was twenty, and I looked about the same—we might have been brothers or comrades. But I might as well have been a child just then.

It hurts, I whimpered, meaning my legs and everything

17

in general. The sounds that left my mouth were mere noises, but Trevyn understood in much the same way that he had always understood.

"I know," he said. "Or I can imagine. . . . Perhaps I cannot. Try to rest as we ride."

He got me onto his horse, carrying me sideways in the saddle before him. We cantered southward along the shore toward the port city of Nemeton with the men taking turns carrying Frain. I settled into a time of numb endurance measured out in the rhythm of the horses' hooves. A memory floated up from deep mind. Trevyn had carried me like this before, but I had been very young then, still in my first fur.

It was dusk before we made the castle. Frain was taken to a sickchamber amid a tumult of excitement caused by our arrival. Trevyn sat me down in front of a blazing fire and saw to it himself that I ate. Then he put me into the royal bed that the lord of that place had meant for him, and he rubbed my strange, stiff limbs with his warm hands until I was able to sleep. It was the first time I had slept between sheets.

He was sitting by my side when I awoke in the morning.

That one I found? I asked.

"Much the same." Trevyn reached out to touch me, awkwardly, for no reason. "Dair, why did you go away?"

I had to. The call was on me.

"And I did not understand or see what was happening to you. So there you were all alone when you needed me most."

You came when I needed you most, I said. He did not reply, and I lay thinking.

The change, I added—*I had to face it alone.*

So here I was in human form. But I was not likely to make a very satisfactory human, I sensed. And my bond brother, what of him? All of life seemed in confusion.

I do not want to leave you again, I said to Trevyn. But we both knew I must.

18

Chapter Two

Being on two legs was a nuisance. It took me several days just to learn to stand and walk without help. The height made me dizzy and made everything look strange. And there were matters of modesty to be dealt with, where to relieve myself and clothing, which was a constant bother. I wore as little as possible. And eating. Luckily I had been accustomed to cooked meats, so it was only the manner of eating that was strange to me. I could no longer put my face down to a plate on the floor. I had to sit and use a cup and convey the food to my mouth with my hands. No mention was made of knife and fork, for which I was grateful. The hands were clumsy enough. So was the mouth.

"Move your lips," Trevyn would say to me gently from time to time. "They are shaped like mine now. Make speech."

"Awaaa," I would say, or perhaps "Rawawarrr." I could manage nothing more. Trevyn would repeat a simple word to me, "meat" or "water," trying to help me. But I could not be helped. I had missed learning something that human young learn while I was a wolf.

For that first week, while I was struggling with human form, the stranger I had found lay abed and did not fully come to himself. He could be roused and given wine and bread and broth, so he grew no weaker. He talked. But he talked only to himself, his dreams or shadows on the wall, and in a language no one could understand. He did not know where he was, the doctors said.

As soon as I could walk the distance I went with Trevyn to see him.

19

He sat propped up on pillows, his hair bright and fine as feathers against the white linen, his crippled left arm beside him and the other folded across his chest. A doctor and servants stood by his bedside shaking their heads. The stranger youth was talking steadily to no one at all. His voice ran like a river between walls, behind weirs, calm, forceful, controlled. He might have been addressing a council. Trevyn sat beside him and listened, frowning.

"I thought I knew every language of the overseas lands," he said, "but this one is new to me."

The youth talked through the afternoon and into the night. The doctor could neither soothe him into slumber nor rouse him to sense. Trevyn kept his seat, trying for some kind of understanding. It was very hard to hear emotion in that level voice. A few times there might have been a hint of anger or plea. And as dark fell I thought I began to hear weariness. No—more than weariness.

"What is it, Dair?" Trevyn asked me. "You have instincts for many things. What do you think ails him?"

Despair—or desperation.

Trevyn nodded and turned to the physician. "Let us try the little yellow flower," he said.

It was called Veran's Crown or Elfin Gold. It had come back to Isle with the other things of wonder, and it grew everywhere, but it was used only with greatest reverence and in cases of sore need, for it was a powerful balm. None was yet in bloom so early in the season, but some was always kept dried in jars. A single dried plant was brought to Trevyn along with steaming water. He whispered the blessing, crushed the tiny thing and dropped it into the water. The sweet green smell of it filled the room, the very smell of peace.

Suddenly I felt that I was a wolf again, a pup, romping by Trevyn's side without a notion of anything except joy and without a care in the world—I could have wept for knowing it would never again be so, but at the same time the memory gave me a feeling of utter gladness. I could almost believe that those days had come back to stay. Those springtime days—the stranger had quieted, seeming to listen for a sound only he could hear. Suddenly he sat straight up and turned to the shadowy figure by his bedside—the light was very low, so as not to trouble him.

"Tirell?" he asked, or rather, he begged. His voice was no longer steady—it shook with emotion.

"Nay," said Trevyn gently, "it is I, Trevyn, King of Isle."

I brought a candle closer so they could see each other. The red-haired youth looked up in confusion.

"Tirell is King of Vale," he said in a dialect we could understand, a mixed mongrel language called Traderstongue. He stared at Trevyn. "Where—I thought I heard Tirell."

"It is the balm," Trevyn told him. "We had to give it to you to—comfort you. It has taken you back to a place of peace, perhaps the home where you were loved as a child."

"Yes—though in truth it was none too peaceful." The youth sank back on his pillows with a sigh, and when he spoke he had found calm again, it must have been second nature to him. "My name is Frain," he said. "If this place has a king, I dare say it is not Ogygia."

"I have never heard it called by that name." Trevyn raised his brows. "We call it Isle. How did you come here, Frain?"

"In a leaky coracle."

We saw you, I said. Frain heard it as a growl. He was not one of the special few who remembered, who could understand me. He gave me a startled, mistrustful look, such as the castlefolk often did.

"That is Dair," Trevyn said. "He who found you by the sea."

"I owe him my thanks, then." Frain looked at me doubtfully and did not offer the thanks he said he owed.

"We found no coracle," Trevyn added after a moment.

"It leaked, and then it sank," Frain said in a matter-of-fact way. "I am not much of a sailor, and I had not carried enough food, either. Your Majesty, I am ravenous."

"We will get you food. Call me Trevyn."

"I can't. Anyone can see you are a True King."

The doctor bustled out to see about the food, and Trevyn sat smiling at Frain in amusement and growing affection. There was an air of fine, gallant bravery about Frain, and yet a modesty as well, so marked that it was almost shyness. An odd blend. I felt my heart go out to him for the oddity of him—well, it had gone out to him before I knew him.

"Why, then," said Trevyn, "call me Lord."

"Thank you, my lord. My brother, Tirell—he is a True King too."

I would not have thought there could be two such kings in the world. This was either madness or the touch of the goddess. Trevyn gave Frain a keen glance. "You mistook me for him a moment ago," he said.

"In the dark." Frain smiled, a warm smile and very good to look on. "You are as comely as he, but his hair is as black as yours is fair, Lord, black as jet, and his face white with scarcely a hint of color to it, and his eyes blazing blue, ice blue. Women pine with longing for him." Frain's smile faded. "But that is the least of him," he added quietly. "I know the power of the True King. This is a magical place, Lord, is it not?"

Trevyn only nodded. I believe he was astonished.

"Then perhaps you can understand," Frain said slowly, "when I say I have met with a peculiar sort of enchantment, or perhaps a doom. I have traveled seven years since I left Vale, my lord, but they have not aged me. I have not aged a day since the day I was foolish enough to bathe in Lady Death's mirroring lake. I was fifteen then, and I am nearly twenty-four now. But I am still fifteen—in effect."

Trevyn had seen too many marvels in his life to doubt anyone. He merely nodded.

"You do not look fifteen," he said with a scholar's interest. "Maybe seventeen or so." Frain was sturdy, muscular even, and handsome in spite of the crippled arm.

"I was well grown." A tinge of bitterness seeped into his voice. "A child in the body of a man."

"And now you have eternal youth." Trevyn sat back, musing, gazing at the stranger. "People judge that to be the greatest of blessings, the foremost gift of the gods."

"They are mistaken." Frain spoke so quietly, so evenly, that the sense of his words struck with a shock, jagged rock under still water. "It is the curse of the gods. Lord, I am entrapped. I have not been able to grow or leave anything behind in all my wanderings. Seven years and they have not helped me or healed me—it is as if I am frozen, a fly in amber. Lord, the wound smarts as if it were given but yesterday."

For a moment there was silence. Even Trevyn did not seem to know what to say. Then the doctor scurried in, leading a servant with a steaming bowl of porridge. Frain could scarcely contain his eagerness. His hand trembled as he reached for the spoon.

"Slowly," Trevyn cautioned, holding the bowl for him.

He ate, and not very slowly. As he sat back after eating we could see that he was in pain.

"Gut-ache," he said. "Sorry. I tried not to gulp."

"Never mind. Lie down." Trevyn helped him to curl up under the blankets. "Keep warm, maybe sleep. I will have someone bring you a warm brick."

"Thank you. Truly, my lord, I feel that I shall soon be much better. Thank you for everything."

He wanted us to leave. But Trevyn lingered, frowning thoughtfully.

"Only one more question, if you do not mind telling me. What were you seeking, that you set to sea in so small a craft, unprovisioned, and in the freezing season yet?"

"Ascalonia," said Frain, his voice muffled by blankets. "Ogygia. The home of the goddess, if you will."

"Is that a sunlit land? You could have gotten to it in a larger vessel, if it is, and at a more clement time of year. Or was it perhaps death you were seeking?"

"Yes, in a sense. Her name is Shamarra. But to find her I must first speak to the goddess in Ogygia." Frain stirred tensely. "I hardly know anymore what I really seek—growth, death, change, ending—"

"Who is Shamarra?"

"That is yet another question." The daring of him, with a king he scarcely knew! But Trevyn smiled and touched his shoulder.

"Sleep well," he said, and we left him.

We did not speak until we reached the far end of the corridor.

He is a marvel, I said finally. I sensed uneasily that he did not like me, and I wished I could abate my liking for him, but I could not.

"Ay," said Trevyn absently. "I expected no less. And it is a good name—can you say it, Dair? FRAIN—just try it one sound at a time. FR—"

Stop it! Sudden, surprising anger snapped through me and I roared aloud, *Let me alone, I am of no use, I am fate's fool, a freak*—The few servants within hearing fled in panic at the noise I was making, but Trevyn hugged me. I stopped my ranting, laid my head on his shoulder and groaned.

"I am sorry," he said. "I won't badger you anymore."

It is not you. The castlefolk talk in front of me as if

I am too stupid to understand them. They call me wood-wouse, wild man. I make such an oaf of a human.

"They are frightened," said Trevyn, and he stepped back a little, eyeing me with a smile. "You are rather awesome, you know. Face of the god of the wild things—I have seen gods, remember—and strength enough for any two men, and grace coming to you already, grace learned from no human. . . ."

Some of the maids beckon at me, as if I were meat for their tasting. Then they laugh at me when I refuse them. I wish I were—I could not say I wished I were dead, though it had a fine ring to it, for it was not true. The Old Language speaks from the heart. It cannot say untruth.

"You wish you were a wolf again?"

There spoke Trevyn True King. He would not flinch from whatever was. I faced him with blinking eyes.

Yes. That is part of it. But the worst of it is—I forced myself onward, floundering after the sour scent of truth—*Frain. He does not like me any better than the others do.*

"He is frightened, too," said Trevyn.

But why? I had expected better of him, somehow.

"The essence of you, the wildness, I think. Because you remind him of something—or because he is frightened of things within himself."

I had thought he would be courageous, I complained.

"He is, he is very courageous! Look at how far he has come. And there is nothing more fearsome than what he is facing."

I did not understand. But Trevyn spoke as one who knew.

"Perhaps he will learn a different sort of valor from you," Trevyn added. "Perhaps that is what he has come here for, to learn from you."

How? I burst out. *I cannot talk to him, I can't read or write, even. Any dog could serve him better. Mother of mercy, what am I to do? He will not want me—*

Trevyn quieted me with a soft glance. We are not very different, you and I, that glance said. We are equals. I stood stunned.

"You will find your way, I am sure of it," he said. "I was a mute, too, for a while, when I was with your mother. Perhaps you are indeed intended to continue what I have begun. Remember the words of the seeress, and await the word of the One."

24

Chapter Three

Frain ate often during the next several days. When he was not eating, and sometimes as he ate, he talked with Trevyn. I would listen.

"Dair is my son," Trevyn explained when he judged it was time. Frain looked both shocked and dubious.

"But how can that be, my lord? Are you older than you seem? I would have said that you two were nearly of the same age."

"Nay, I am just twenty. And Dair was born only two years ago. He was a wolf. They mature faster than human young," said Trevyn offhandedly. "There was some magic involved," he added after a moment.

"I should think so." Frain stared hard at me, his face like a mask. "Well, there is magic in Vale as well, though it is a harsher magic than what I sense here, and there were creatures there that were half beast, and I was not afraid of them—"

"Magic, on the mainland?" Trevyn interrupted eagerly.

"I never really thought of Vale as part of the mainland."

He spoke of Vale at some length. It was a place apart, turned inward upon itself because of the mountains that ringed it all around. It was ruled by canton kings and a high kingship of sacred monarchs who often went mad. Frain's foster brother Tirell was the son of one such king. Two things became clear as Frain spoke: one, that he loved his brother Tirell with a wolf's love, unquestioning. And the other, that Tirell had gone insane and hurt him badly. It was Tirell who had crippled his arm.

On top of that there was the matter of his fostering,

of which he had been ignorant, that he had been given away at birth by his own parents. And on top of that there was the matter of Shamarra.

She was very beautiful with a delicate beauty, like crystal, pure and apart, like clear water. "She was the lake," Frain explained. "Or the—being of the lake, the goddess of the lake. And the lake is very deep and shadowy and still, a hidden thing, it lies amid the mountains of death, what we call Acheron, where no one ever goes."

We have seen it, I said. Trevyn glanced at me sharply to hush me, for Frain found my voice disturbing. It took him some while to go on.

He had fallen into ardent love with Shamarra. He had looked into her lake without terror, bathed in it without being dragged down by dark fingers. Thus, all unawares, he had won his immortality. But Shamarra had loved Tirell—I heard the hard undertug of anger in Frain's voice, nearly hidden by the smooth surface flow of his words—though Tirell wanted only to avoid her. In the end she had offered herself to him, and in his madness he had taken her, savagely.

Raped her? The goddess? Did he really mean that? The words should have been cried out in rage or shock, but they were not. Neither of us knew how to answer Frain's unnatural calm. He stared back at us for a while and then turned away.

"She went away dishonored, with her hair streaming down over her face," he said, and he would talk no more that day.

How Trevyn knew it of Frain, I am not sure, but it was true. Frain was frightened of the savagery within, of that which comes out in dark and dreams.

Though I had gone human, I was still a night creature by nature, napping by day, restless after dark. I roamed the castle when other folk were abed. And that night as I roamed I met with Frain. He was naked, for all folk slept naked in those days, and one glance told me he was not himself. His fair and gentle face was set in dangerous lines, and he walked like a beast that stalks its prey. As I watched, he crouched and crept his way to the great hall, and from the wall behind the dais he took a long smiting sword, an ornament that had not been used in years—well, there was no need in Isle. Then he stood there with the weapon in his one good hand and his withered arm dangling. He had to lean against the sword's weight and contort himself for balance. He stood hearkening, but when I made a noise he did not hear me. He was in some other place.

"Tirell," he breathed into the darkness. "Come and meet your doom, Tirell, for what you have done to me. Fabron, you deceiving bastard—"

Fabron was his father who had given him away. Frain stood taut and naked holding the great sword, cursing Fabron and Tirell with every sort of punishment he or his gods could visit on them. The hatred in those curses chilled me, that and the blind stare of those clear brown eyes in the night. I fled to get Trevyn.

"Sleepwalking," he said as soon as I had told him about Frain. He came with me, lacing his breeches as we ran. "He has been having trouble sleeping, so tonight they gave him a draught, and now he is sleeping with a vengeance. Where is he?"

Frain had left the great hall. After a few minutes we found him prowling catlike down one of the corridors. "Tirell, you coward, where are you?" he asked the night. The tone was full of threat. The sword was raised.

"I have to disarm him," Trevyn said. "Dair, go get me one of the wooden practice swords from the barracks."

He'll slice it right off, I protested.

"I think not. That sword is old, dull of edge. A wooden sword will do."

I brought it as quickly as I was able. Even so, Frain had stalked through a quarter of the castle by the time I got back, with Trevyn never far from his side, warning the guards out of his way. Frain had come out to a platform when I found them. Trevyn and a cluster of guards whispered nearby. Frain stood, no longer the coolheaded hunter, his anger pulsing hot, blood heat.

"Tirell!" He shouted the challenge, it rang from the stone walls. He had forgotten Fabron, it seemed.

Trevyn took the wooden sword from me and stepped forward to meet him. At the first touch of the mock blade to his own, Frain lunged forward, filled with lust to kill.

"Mothers!" Trevyn exclaimed, but it was not Frain's passion that surprised him. Frain was a master swordsman.

He was splendid, deadly. Even I could see that. The guards gasped, watching him. Trevyn was skillful, he had been well trained, but weapons had never been his main love. Dreaming had, and peace. There was no room for dreaming in that night.

"What am I to do with him?" Trevyn wondered aloud, breathing hard.

He had two good hands, and Frain had only one. Trevyn was trying to engage Frain's sword with his wooden one while he used his other hand to wrench it away. But it was all he could do to parry Frain's blows, far less get hold of that hilt. Frain was lightning fast, brilliant, murderous. Trevyn could not stand his ground. He gave way, circling back, feeling for advantage.

"Coward," Frain taunted.

Hardly a coward, who faced him with a mock weapon. The guards eyed each other, wondering if they could help Trevyn without breach of honor, without hurting his pride.

"Surround him, you fellows," Trevyn panted, forgetting pride for the time.

The guards moved to obey. But before they reached Frain the wooden sword broke with a horrible snap. I shouted with fear—Frain's sword flashed straight for Trevyn's head! He fell. But as the guards lunged forward a movement of his hand stopped them. And Frain stood still and lowered his long sword, breathed one last curse and walked away.

Trevyn waited until he was well down the corridor before he got up.

I thought you were as good as dead! I told him, shaking. There was a welt on his head. He smiled at me.

"Praise be, I caught the flat of it. And Frain is satisfied with his revenge. At least I hope he is."

He was. He went back to his bed and fell sound asleep. Some time later we slipped in and stole the sword away from him to take it back where it belonged. Trevyn went to see him first thing the next morning.

"What happened to you?" Frain demanded, staring. There was a bright red mark across the left side of Trevyn's forehead.

"I lost a bout to a better," Trevyn said wryly. "How are you? Did you sleep well?"

"I—no. Please, my lord, no more draughts. I slept, but I had the most—terrible dream."

"No more draughts," Trevyn agreed readily, seating himself. "What was the dream?"

"I—" Frain looked down, uncomfortable. "I was—quarreling with my brother."

"Oh?" said Trevyn, prodding for better truth. Quarreling was hardly the word.

"Really, my lord, it was nothing, it was of no significance. Dreams are unaccountable things." Frain looked quite pained. Trevyn had mercy on him, or a partial mercy.

"This brother of yours—you say he is a True King, and yet he ravished your beloved, crippled you—"

"He was not himself," Frain said hotly. "If you knew what he had gone through—" He would have sprung to sword for Tirell's sake, I felt sure of it. How odd! He who had been ready to kill him a few hours before—

"The suffering comes before the kingship," Trevyn remarked.

"Yes." Frain gave Trevyn a wondering glance, all his heat cooled. "Yes, my lord, you know, you understand. I—remember how he wept after he had wounded me. Then I fainted, and by the time I awoke he had come back from madness, he was better, truly better, warm and whole as I had not known him to be since—since it had started. He was the brother I had always loved. He took my hand and met my eyes with love and sorrow, and the land itself hailed him, and all the people were rejoicing because the blessing of the goddess was on him—"

"So how could you be so petty as to sulk about a little thing like an arm?" Trevyn put in dryly.

"An arm and a true love." Frain tried to match Trevyn's tone and his smile, but could not. "I went away," he added.

"To find Ogygia and lay your case before the goddess."

"No, that came later. First I went to the lake to find Shamarra. But everything had changed. The swan had gone black and was as crippled as I, and the water itself was fearsome. When I looked in I saw—never mind." His eyes shifted and he hastened on. "There was a woman there, a sort of queenly goddess, and she told me that the wrath of Adalis was on Shamarra because of her overweening. She had been transformed into a night bird and sent to wander the wind."

Trevyn looked both startled and intense. "What did you say is the name of your goddess?"

"There are many names. Every woman's name is a name of the goddess. There is Eala the swan and the white horse Epona, and Morrghu the raven of war, and

29

Vieyra the hell hag, and Suevi, Rae, Mela—dozens of others. But the mother of Vale is Adalis."

"I thought you said that. I heard, but I could not believe my ears." Trevyn put a palm to his hurt brow with a sigh. "Frain, if you can say that most holy name so off-handedly without the castle stones flying from their places and raining destruction on your head, truly you must be of immortal kind."

"Really?" Frain said that softly, but his excitement grew as he talked, he leaned forward and his voice rose. "You mean you call her by that same name, and she is here, she can respond to you? Do you really mean that?"

"She is here as much as anywhere," Trevyn said with some small wonder, for the goddess makes every land her own.

"Why, then," Frain breathed, "this must be Ogygia after all."

"Perhaps. If you say so. I am surprised that it has taken you so long to find it."

"Have you ever tried to find a legendary land?" Frain asked, a hint of vexation in his steady voice. "I never knew there were so many lands that lay beyond Vale. I trudged across them, places and places of them, and no one had ever heard of Ogygia, all they could do was point me toward this one and that one who might know, and I asked them all to no avail. Follow the setting sun, they said, and find the ocean. And when I found it at last, I walked the length of that vast shoreline looking for Ogygia or news of Ogygia. And I had never seen an immensity like that of the sea." Frain's voice was tinged with awe and terror. "I knew when I saw it that it was as the woman by the lake had said, that I could no sooner reach Ogygia than the crippled swan. But I had to try."

Trevyn sighed in vexation of his own. He had indeed been to legendary lands, and he badly wanted to explain to Frain the ways of the All-Mother. But he knew that Frain had to find her on his own.

"There is an island far, far west of here," he said finally, "where the elves have made their home, the ancient folk. There I spoke with the goddess once on her mountain of the moon. The name of that island is Elwestrand. Wild swans fly there. But you cannot go there unless she sends one of her swimming ships for you."

Frain's face sagged. "Why, it sounds as if I must go there nevertheless," he whispered.

"I think not. But we will speak to her soon and see what she has to say to you."

"Where? How?" Frain rose to his feet in his excitement, and Trevyn could not help smiling.

"As soon as the weather has broken and you are strong. In a suitable place. Patience!"

Chapter Four

The thaw came, and then the early spring sun. Catkins sprouted on the twigs. Frain felt ready to travel, so on a bright morning we made our way out of Nemeton. Trevyn and Frain rode in cavalcade and I walked by Trevyn's side. Once out of town, on the wealds, they put their horses to the trot, and I ran. I had learned to run again, on two legs now, and it felt glorious to be out in the air again, reveling in the tangle of lusty springtime smells and the feel of strong limbs—but my speed was pitiful compared to what it once had been.

I can barely keep up, I complained to Trevyn, and he slowed the pace.

"By human standards," he said, "you are an extraordinary runner. Certainly the fastest I have ever seen."

Having only two legs is a bother, I mourned.

"Well, then, ride, as I do. You will have four again."

I faced the prospect doubtfully. Even my own human height was still sometimes dizzying to me, and the horse was higher yet. Still, I knew they could not always be waiting for me.

"Or share a mount with me," Trevyn added.

I felt Frain's chilly glance on me. At once pride took over, and I got on a horse of my own. I learned to ride within a few minutes. It was not hard. I had only to keep my balance and try to come to agreement with the steed. I spoke to the horse as I would to any fellow creature, and I never learned a man's way of dominating it. No matter. We rode pleasantly. By midmorning we crested the uplands and paused to look back on Nemeton. We could see for miles the course of the deep river that flowed down from the Great Eastern Forest, and just beyond the city we could see anchorage and the masts of ships and the gray glint of the sea. But we turned our backs on the sea for the time, riding toward the north and west.

We were going to a place just at the southern skirts of the Forest, a place where the river forked and formed a sort of island, where there was a sacred grove. The Wyrdwood, it was called. If the goddess had to be summoned she was more likely to come amiably there than anywhere else in Isle.

I grew to enjoy riding over the next few days. It was indeed rather like having four legs again. I think Frain liked riding too. He needed only one hand to hold the reins, and he could do it as well as anyone. In fact, he rode as well as Trevyn. It was not hard to tell that he had been a prince, that he had been born to ride. But he would not wear a sword. Trevyn had brought him one with a cloak when we were making ready, and he had refused it.

"The shield arm won't work for me anymore. I have no defense," he said, shrugging. "I do better to stay out of trouble."

Trevyn had raised his brows at this talk of defenselessness, but of course he could not tell Frain he knew better. "It is only for show in Isle anyway," he had said. "Wear it. You are of rank."

"I gave up both rank and swordsmanship some years ago," Frain had said.

So he rode swordless. What an oddling he was. I did not care, I liked him. There was the bond on us, but I liked him for himself as well. Alas, he felt no such liking for me. He stiffened with discomfort when I rode beside him.

"*Nille tha riste,* Dair," Trevyn told me privately. "Do not despair."

We came to the holy grove on the third day. Trevyn led us in, and the trees loomed above us, hushed and mighty. That place was full of magic, anyone could feel it. All the magic in Isle centered there. Frain rode steadily, and I knew once again that he was brave, for more than one man of the company went pale with fear. The retainers were afraid to look behind them, knowing that they would see no way out, that the grove we had just entered would seem to go on pathless and forever. Trevyn saw their terror and had them stop.

"Wait here," he told them. "We three will go on to the center alone."

So Frain and Trevyn and I rode down the spiraling spaces between the giant boles. Trevyn knew the way quite surely. He sensed the center. It drew him, it was in him. He had been born here, in a way.

The center was only a circle of green meadow around a young and growing tree. A unicorn grazed there. It moved off when it saw us, its solitude disturbed. White flowers that looked like lacework grew there. The tree was in new leaf, and the leaves were jade green and amethyst, sapphire, ruby red and tourmaline red and topaz. They glowed in the sunlight, and they sent flakes of it skimming across the grass at every stir of the breeze.

"This is her tree," Trevyn said.

We got down and let the horses graze. "Alys!" Trevyn called, not loudly. "Mother of us all, come to us, if you please."

"What was that you called her?" Frain whispered.

"Her sooth-name." Trevyn barely glanced at him, for he was listening, alert. "Not so very different from your name for her."

"You think it is the same goddess?"

"How can it be otherwise? There is only one goddess, despite the many names. And she is only one aspect of the One who has no name," he added. "Alys!" he called again, and then we sat on the grass. We sat until nightfall and on into the forest night which is all shadow and no light. From time to time through the long wait Frain glanced doubtfully at Trevyn. He sat undisturbed, and Frain sat as well.

With night came the goddess. She was only a rustle of breeze at first. Then a cool voice spoke from the neighborhood of the sacred tree. "Alberic," she asked, for that was Trevyn's true-name, "what do you want?"

"A favor for a friend, Lady," said Trevyn to the voice. It was no use flattering the goddess or being less than forthright with her.

"Ask anything you like for yourself, King of Isle, but ask nothing for your friend. He does not know me." She sounded annoyed. "You have summoned me here—"

"It is for myself, Alys, for my heart has gone out to him. Help him. Please."

34

"He has no wisdom. He is no better than a child."

"As I was when you first knew me. If he is ignorant, then he needs your guidance the more. Mother, he has felt the touch of your hand, I know he has."

Frain sat by himself, trembling at the strangeness of the voice in the night and not able to understand what was being said, for of course Alys and Trevyn spoke in the Old Language. I wanted to go to Frain, but I knew he would take no comfort from my closeness.

Alys sighed, a breath of wind.

"Alberic, you greathearted nuisance—" she said, and there was a puff of red light, red as fire, and the most horrible of hags confronted us from midair. It struck terror into me, I felt my sweat run, and it wrung a stifled scream from Frain.

"The Lady is out of humor," Trevyn said tightly in Traderstongue, speaking to Frain. "She is not usually so— unlovely."

"He knows that," Alys snapped. In quick succession she took form as swan, red roe deer, raven, white horse, and a woman holding three red apples in her hands. She was blonde, gray eyed, grave. "Adalis," Frain whispered.

"I am all of these and more," Alys acknowledged. Suddenly a shimmering beauty stood in the night, a woman who shone like running water, her hair a silky torrent of silvergold, her soft green robe flowing to her feet. Frain jumped up with a cry. "Shamarra!" he gasped, but as he moved the vision shifted shape. A ragged brown bird stood there instead.

"Why did you do it to her, why!" Frain shouted, sobbing, plunging forward. But on the instant the bird stretched hugely, horribly, a nightmare thing, it was a feathered serpent rippling up over our heads, then something with horns, then something with a woman's laughing, shrieking head—all fast, too fast to fathom. It hissed and writhed and menaced, sending Frain staggering back with the shock of it. I caught him as he nearly fell, and in an instant Trevyn was beside us as well, and the goddess laughed and laughed in the night.

"Why does she laugh?" Frain asked Trevyn from between clenched teeth.

"She says you are a fool to think Shamarra still stands and weeps."

More words came as the goddess's amusement calmed somewhat.

"She says Shamarra is not one to weep for long. Did she not send her minions against Tirell even before you left Vale, overstepping her authority? She was punished, but at this very moment she coldly plans her more fitting and lasting revenge. Frain, beware, Alys says. Shamarra makes a puissant enemy."

"But Shamarra is not my enemy!" Frain cried. "She is my beloved!"

The goddess had quieted and taken her most fair and simple form, a moonlike orb, pearly white. It flared briefly in warning, white fire, and Trevyn put an arm around Frain.

"She says you are your own worst enemy. Hush, do not argue, listen. She speaks."

She told us the tale of the crippled swan, and as she did so Trevyn told it to Frain in words he could understand.

In ancient times in Vale, it seemed, there had been two princes, twins, one light and one dark. They were sons of the goddess. And the light one was raised as the king's favored son, and he was called Doray, meaning Golden. But the dark one was taken as an infant to Acheron and left there to die. The All-Mother in form of Eala the swan took pity on him and gathered him under her wing, and he lived.

Doray knew nothing of his brother. But in an inner sense he always missed him, and he grew up warmthless and fey. One day when he was yet small he tore from his nurse's grasp and hurled himself over the battlements. He survived the fall, but it left him with a crippled, useless arm. "I was only trying to fly," he said.

The king's vassals would not accept the odd, crippled boy as heir, and when Doray was a youth they rose up against his father and him. The king was killed and Doray fled to Acheron, where he knew no one would follow him. He walked through the twisted trees and climbed the crags of despair. He came to the dark lake and stepped into it, and because he was of immortal sort he became a swan, a fair swan white as asphodel, white as white lotus. But his wing hung useless in the water, and still he could not fly. A black reflection looked back at him from the water.

"Who are you?" he asked it.

"I am Arget," the black swan replied, "your brother, whom you have never known. Search for me."

"But how can you be my brother, you who are black?"

"Search for me," Arget said.

36

Doray left the lake and was human once more.

So he went on yet again, through the forest of fear, up the barrier mountains. In time he found a youth sleeping—it was Arget. A warm feeling went through him that he had never known. He awakened him, and they embraced.

They wandered, befriending each other. When they felt the bond complete, they made their way back to the dark and mirroring lake. Both stepped in together. Then a single white swan floated there, and its image in the water, white, and its wing was well and whole.

"You can fly now," Arget said from the lake, the reflection said. "I am at one with you now, as I ought to be. Fly."

The goddess grew still. The tale was done.

"Did he fly away?" Frain asked after a silence.

"Who knows? The tale is your own, Frain, and you will show us the end to it."

"But how so?" Frain creased his brow in puzzlement. "Do I have a brother of whom I know nothing?"

"The dark twin, the one within. You have seen him."

Frain shuddered and seemed to shrink back. "What does all this have to do with Shamarra?" he asked.

"Little enough."

"But—"

"Shamarra wants nothing but vengeance," the goddess warned. "And your love of her means nothing, not even protection, for you will not be able to face her until you have touched the opposing threads of your own life."

Trevyn translated that with some difficulty. "Threads?" Frain murmured in bewilderment when he was done.

"As on the loom," the goddess said impatiently. "Must I explain everything? No good will come to you until dog meets wolf. You are but a puppy now, in puppy love—is it truly Shamarra you seek?"

The question caused Frain some unease. He stood breathing heavily. "If Shamarra is death, yes," he said at last.

"Shamarra is danger, but your death will not be so easy to come by. You are an immortal, by your own folly, and your destiny is woven into the pattern. Shamarra is an aspect of Vieyra the hag who is a form of my being which is a mask worn by the nameless One who is infinite—and you are the merest thread in the cloak of the infinite, Frain. You are a fleck, a cloud wisp, a leaf floating on the turning tide, no more."

He stood silent.

"No, Frain, it is your own deliverance you seek," Alys said in tones of boredom, the moonlike circle of light said, faintly pulsing.

"Shamarra—" Frain began. He must have been bewitched to cleave so to thoughts of Shamarra.

"She does not care about you," the goddess snapped. "And she will squash you like a fly if you come between her and her prey. Now listen, if you are to be of any use."

"Use to whom?" Frain asked warily.

"Such temerity." The goddess did not sound amused. "Listen, I say. When fire weds with flood, redemption will come to you, no sooner. When you have known the power of the fern flower, it will come to you. That is your quest. Go now."

"But where?"

"East." The moonform of the goddess dimmed into dusk, then darkness. "Maeve and Dair will help you," added a voice in the night. A breeze blew, and then all was silent.

"But where is Shamarra?" Frain cried out. There was no answer, and he turned away from the tree that stood unseen somewhere in the night, his one good hand clenched into a fist, trying to contain his fury.

"The one question I have come all this way to ask her," he panted, and then his anger choked him and he could not go on.

"From what the goddess said, you would do well to stay far from Shamarra," Trevyn remarked.

"I will not believe she is my enemy," said Frain. "Can not, will not." Anger had left his tone to be replaced by a dead and settled desperation that I for one found far more fearsome. What ailed him, that he would not heed the word of the goddess? Trevyn put an arm around him, as if to warm the cold enchantment that was on him.

"You will not be able to sleep until you have vented your rage," he said. "Shout, weep, pound on me, something."

"I am seldom able to sleep in any event." Frain shrugged off the embrace, gently but sulkily. "Can we be gone from here?" he asked.

"In the pitch dark? Well, why not?" Trevyn liked challenges. "Dair, what is needed to roam the night?"

A good nose.

"You lead, then."

We blundered off with the horses trailing after us. But I could not find the way. It was Trevyn's grove, and I was not he. Also, my mind was in an uproar. Maeve and I were to help Frain, Alys had said, Maeve my mother who lived across the sea. Frain and I would voyage on that sea, just as Trevyn had said—

I will go with him, I said aloud, and I banged right into a massive tree.

"What is it?" Frain called sharply, startled. He had heard only a thump and a growl in the night. But Trevyn had heard me well enough.

"Let us stop here," he said in a tight voice.

"All right." Frain sounded his gentle self again, and sheepish. "It is no use running away like a whipped child. My lord Trevyn, I am truly grateful to you for all you have done for me."

"Others have helped me when I needed it." Trevyn sat on the ground, and we did the same. "Well, Frain, I will have a ship prepared for you."

"What is the use?" Frain lay back on the soft loam. "I still don't know where I am going."

"East. To Tokar. To see Maeve. And may you fare better in that country than I did."

"Who is Maeve?"

My mother, I said. She whom I remembered only as milk and warm fur—

"Dair's mother. A sorceress. Could you sleep now? You should be quite exhausted."

I believe Trevyn must have put some small spell on him, for as if he needed only the suggestion Frain rolled to one side and fell into the slumberer's rhythm of gentle breathing. Trevyn put a cloak over him and turned to me.

"So," he whispered, "the pattern is plain to you."

I knew—I felt the bond. Even before the goddess spoke my name with his.

"I know, I know it well enough. I had ordered myself not to interfere, but I can't help telling you, Dair—I will miss you."

I found my way to him in the dark and touched his shoulder. It was hard, as if he held himself clenched against pain. He turned to me at the touch and embraced me fiercely.

"I only hope he will learn to love you as I do," he muttered, then hastily let go of me. "Sleep," he told me.

I lay down and pretended to sleep to please him. He sat with his head against a tall kerm-oak tree, drawing on the strength of the god, the grove. After a while he lay down as well, but I do not think he slept any more than I did. In the morning he silently found us our horses and led us back to the others, and then out of the Wyrdwood.

Chapter Five

Once we were back in Nemeton, Trevyn set about finding a ship for the crossing to Tokar. Frain was startled by the news that I was coming with him.

"To see his mother?" he demanded.

"I think there is more to it than that," Trevyn told him.

His honesty would not let him graciously accept me as his traveling companion, but there was no way he could graciously refuse, either—not when he was sailing on Trevyn's ship and I was Trevyn's son. I went to see him the next day, to try to come to an understanding with him.

He was in his chamber, putting in order the piles of gifts and clothing people had given him. He was the castle favorite—he had such a gentle, honest way about him, he was the sort of youth that maidens smiled on without a second thought, that mothers trusted with their virgin daughters. He had a knack for making friends with everyone except me, it seemed. I knocked on his open door and he turned to see me standing there.

"Dair!" he exclaimed. "Come—in. . . ." He sounded none too sure of the welcome. I came in anyway, went to him and knelt, placing my clasped hands in his in the ritual gesture of fealty. It was the only way I could think of to show him that I had given my loyalty to him. His face went white, and he trembled.

"Dair," he said between clenched teeth, "I am—I thank you, but—I am terrified of you."

I rose, stepped back and cupped my hands, a sign of

peace. *Why?* I asked him. It was only an inquiring whine but for once he understood me.

"I wish I knew. I never thought I was such a coward. Dair, I know you mean me all good and no harm, and yet I shake at the sight of you, and I hate myself for it."

Would it help if I wore clothes? I asked, but it was only a senseless muttering to him.

"I swear, I am going to go as mad as Tirell," he said wildly to the air and the walls. "He was afraid of the beast and the brown man, but he found courage to embrace them— and I have none." He edged away from me as if he were going to bolt, but then Trevyn happened in. Frain strode to his side in three steps, and Trevyn looked at him in mild surprise.

"You don't need my protection," he said.

"I know! It is ridiculous. What am I going to do with this fear?" Frain appealed to him.

"See it through."

"It looks as if I am going to have to." Frain stood still, trying to calm himself. Trevyn sat heavily on the bed.

"I have your ship manned and provisioned. You can go with the tide."

Frain stared at him, sensing pain in the calm words. "Lord," he said, "I have no desire to take him from you, believe me."

"I believe it," said Trevyn wryly. He turned to me. "Dair, you had better get some clothes on. Salt spray hard on the skin."

"I need no companion," Frain protested. "For seven years I have walked alone—"

"You need him worse than you know," Trevyn said. I went out, and what they said after that I do not know.

Trevyn walked us down to the harbor when the tide came in. He gave Frain good wishes and the handclasp of an equal. Then he gathered me into a long embrace. Both our faces were wet. Frain stood by, looking abashed.

"I wish you were coming with us," he said at last to Trevyn.

"So do I. But I am a king now, wed, with a child, and as soon as you are gone I will be on my way back to Laueroc. My voyaging days are over." He stood back as we boarded ship. "Farewell, you two!"

Laifrita thae, Dounamir, I called to him. *Sweet peace to thee, my father.* The elfin greeting served for parting.

42

as well. I had never spoken to him so formally, but I knew I would not be coming back.

"Farewell," said Frain.

With a creaking of spars and planks the ship took us down the harbor mouth with the tide. Trevyn stood watching us go. He looked very small, standing on the wharf by the gray water's edge.

Within a few hours after we left port I was dismally seasick. It was no wonder—my own human height still made me queasy sometimes, and the slight rolling of the ship on the calm sea undid me. I could scarcely bear to move. I kept to my bed in the dark hold, lay there and retched and groaned. Though I hardly thought so at the time, it was probably the best thing I could have done. Frain could not very well be afraid of me when I was lying so sick and helpless.

At first he let me alone. But as he saw I was not going to get over my illness in a day or two he began bringing me gruels and things, at first out of duty and later, I think, with real concern. "Try to keep it down," he would say, offering me a plate of some kind of awful mush. No matter what it was, it looked vile to me. I would try to eat it even so, to please him, and then I would give it back the wrong way. He would sigh, clean up the mess and depart. He tried me on wine and all sorts of things, and none of them did any good. This went on for several days, until I felt weak enough to die.

I can't bear this, I said, though I knew he would not understand me. *Three more weeks yet—*

"It can't last much longer," he said, as if he had understood after all. "It will soon run its course."

He brought a basin of water and tried to bathe me. He had managed to warm it somehow, even. I had never been one for much bathing, as I suppose he could see, but I felt too wretched to protest. I lay and let him run the cloth over me, and every once in a while a soft sound would escape my lips. I scarcely noticed when he stopped his sloshings and lavings, muttering to himself fervidly. I scarcely noticed when he laid something on my chest and placed his hand on top of it. But when the slight weight stayed there for some time I made the painful effort to open my eyes.

Frain was standing over me, looking desperate. The thing on my chest was the iron knife he always wore at

43

his belt. I saw, wondering but without alarm, for with tight-lipped concentration he took away his hand and laid it on my forehead, pressing gently. I felt the tremor of effort in that hand. For a long moment he held it there. Then he jerked it away, cursing quietly. He turned toward the wall, his shoulders bent and askew, and I made an inquiring sound.

"Dair?" He looked over to see me looking back at him. He smiled darkly and came to get his knife off my chest.

"Old habits are hard to break," he joked, his voice tight. "I was trying to heal you. I used to be a healer, long ago, before—before I got hurt."

Something in my silence helped him to go on.

"There is a power in metal and in the sons of metal-smiths," he explained. "I could take anything made of iron, a knife blade or whatever, and lay it on together with my hands, and the power would flow through me. I thought maybe—" He stopped with a shrug. "The power is gone," he said after a moment. "I cannot heal anyone anymore, and least of all myself."

I gazed at him, my own woes forgotten. I signaled my interest with voice and gesture, urging him to say more. He sighed and sat on the stool by my bedside. A long silence followed.

"It's not just the hands," he said finally. "It's not just that—Tirell has crippled me. Everything went together, power, prowess, happiness—I've become crippled some other way, somehow. Something inside is hurt. My father lost his healer's power to greed and shame, he told me. Well, I don't know the name of the thing that has taken hold of mine, but it has an ugly face."

He got up abruptly and went out, and I went to sleep.

I felt better. Perhaps the seasickness had run its course, but I think Frain had helped me. Not that there had been any mystic power of healing in his touch, but just that he had cared enough to try—I had seen what effort it had cost him to try. And he had trusted me enough to talk to me. I felt better.

Fran brought me broth in the morning, and I kept it down. And I kept down the sops and slops he brought me thereafter. And a few days later I got up from my bed and wobbled out on deck. The sailors grinned at me and let me alone. Frain stood by me in awkward silence.

"I am glad you are better," he said finally, and I felt

he could not have said it if it were not to some extent true.

He was still distant with me, still put off. But he talked to me more easily and more often as the days went by. He was tense and unhappy, for he liked the sea no better than I did, and the sailors knew it and baited him about it. So he was lonely, and even a mute woodwouse of a companion served better than none. We passed the time with simple games, naughts and crosses, dice and the like. And he would talk about Tirell—how he had loved Tirell. Doglike devotion, folk call it. And he had loved his father Fabron as well, though more as an equal—and Vale itself, his homeland, he spoke of it with longing and love. One day when we had a bit of charcoal at hand he drew me a crude map of Vale on the ship's deck.

"Mountains all around. The river runs down from the northern ones, the dragon range, where there are snow-caps, and empties into a cavern under the king's range to the south and east. No one knows where it goes after that. No one comes into Vale and hardly anyone goes out of it. Those few who do leave, like myself, are as good as dead to those within. I doubt if I will ever wander back."

I only half listened, staring at the rough oval he had drawn on the planking. In a moment I took the charcoal from him and put my own map beside his. It was very nearly the same shape. Clumsily, for I still found it awkward to use my hands, I showed the river running down from the north and west—dragons lived in those parts in the old days, legend said—and I put a dot at the river's mouth—Nemeton. Glancing up at Frain, I saw that he did not understand. How to show him that this was an island, an oval surrounded by sea? I drew a sort of walnut shell with stick masts at Nemeton harbor—a ship.

"Isle?" Frain asked, astonished.

I nodded.

"But—great goddess, what a coincidence! Are they both nearly the same size?"

They were. We discussed it in our way, he figuring weeks of travel and I agreeing. It would take just about a year to make the rounds of either kingdom with any ease.

"And Trevyn and Tirell, True Kings," Frain muttered, more to the air than to me. "So alike, and yet so different. I believe the old woman is playing tricks on me again."

45

He strode off, and that was the end of our one-sided colloquy for that day.

I grew stronger quickly, even on shipboard fare, and I grew more hopeful daily, for Frain was most surely more at ease with me, and maybe one day he might truly be my friend. He grew somewhat more candid with me. One day toward the end of the voyage he asked me a stark question.

"Dair, were you really a wolf for a while?"

I nodded.

"Maybe we are what the goddess meant by wolf meeting dog. People used to call me Puppydog in Vale. . . . Because your mother was a wolf when you were born?"

Nod.

"Swans and serpents," he breathed. "She must be a potent sorceress."

I shrugged in wary agreement. Frain stared at me and then past me, thinking hard.

"Though why that should bother me, I don't know," he said finally. "I've seen enough strange things in my life, especially in a certain lake." He shuddered slightly. "Dair," he burst out, "if you would smile once in a while, it would help."

Trevyn had told me that my expression was fixed and unnerving. The muscles of my face did not work as they usually did in humans, it seemed. But certainly I was willing to try them, I wanted only to please. I flexed my lips. Frain gave me a startled look and glanced quickly away.

"No good. You're baring your teeth," he said quite gently. "Never mind, it was a stupid idea." He rested his elbow on his knee and his head on his hand. A large wave splashed over the ship's railing and drenched him, and he jumped up, cursing.

"Go ahead, douse me!" he shouted at it. "Who am I, anyway? A leaf on the tide, cloud feather, bird dropping or some such. First I search seven years in one direction, and then she sends me back in the other—" His anger turned to a sort of desperate amusement, and he lapsed into laughter, watching the water trickle away from him like tears. "Dair, I'm all wet."

I rose, offering to get him dry clothes, and he followed me below, still softly laughing. Then he stopped with a sigh. "I hate this endless water," he said.

All I could do was hand him dry clothes.

"I never used to be so full of the mubblefubbles," he told me wryly. "So fearful, so bitter—but the days when I was—when I was myself—seem so long ago that I can hardly remember them."

The voyage drifted on. Every morning we sailed blind, straight for the rising sun. Finally one day a rim of black showed below the sun, and the next day cliffs loomed up. We had come to the rocky coast of northern Tokar. It was all wilderness—no towns or homesteads were there.

It was a shock to me, I admit it, that first landsight. I had always lived under the mantle of Trevyn's magic, and I had not known how drab the shadowed world would be. Rocks and twisted trees—without being anything less it was all somehow shrunken, there was no dream in this place. The greens were not the true dream green, the manycolors did not inhabit the tree trunks, the rocks would never sing or roses bloom in the snow or frost-flowers in the heat. It was a sere and unfriendly place even by mainland standards, I suppose, and to my eyes it seemed full of ill omen.

"I hope we are not taken by slavers, as Trevyn was," Frain said.

We fetched our packs of gear and victuals as the ship turned broadside to the coast and sailed along it, searching for a landfall for us. The cliffs looked sheer, but after a while we sighted a jagged ravine where a stream ran down to the ocean. The smallboat was lowered to take us ashore.

Half an hour later we stood on a spit of gravel beach and watched the ship sail away toward Isle, leaving us behind. For the first time I felt desolate.

"Well, Dair," Frain said, "now we're on our own." But he had been on his own for years, without even mute me for company. Was he sensing how I felt?

I turned my back on the sea and looked toward the mainland.

Trevyn had told me where Maeve's home lay. It was somewhere in the jagged ridge country, at the end of the trail that led northward from Jabul. Its tall trees stood like an island in the scrub. We were coming at it from the west, but I felt confident I could find it. The house was encircled by a haunt, an invisible barrier of fear that kept it safe from the brigands and robbers who roamed these wilds. A haunt was a special place. We would be sure to hear talk of it—

47

If the brigands did not do us in first. Neither of us bore any weapon to speak of. Frain had his iron knife, which we would need for cooking and the like, but he had steadfastly refused to take a sword. And as for me, I was human, but not so human as to have mastered the arts of combat.

We filled our water flasks at the stream and climbed the ravine, dragging our packs behind us. Then we silently shouldered them and set off eastward.

Chapter Six

Within a few days I had put away hope of reaching my mother's dwelling before midsummer. There was the heat, to start with. We had not reckoned with such heat so early in the season, or at least I had not. It sapped us. I soon shed all possible clothing. Frain seemed more used to the heat than I, but he could not manage the terrain very well with only one usable arm. The land was rugged, always putting barriers in our way. I cut a staff for each of us, for use as a weapon as well as for help with the rough going. But Frain found his staff as much hindrance as help, and I often had to carry it for him.

Our second day in Tokar we happened on a sort of trail, only the faintest of paths, it might have been made by deer. We followed it gratefully. But we had not been on it more than a quarter of an hour when I sensed danger. I got Frain by the arm and pushed him into a tangle of grapevines, where we crouched in silence. Soon three rough-looking men passed by us close enough to touch, towing some poor unfortunate behind them by a rope. They were slavers. We kept to our cover until they were well gone.

"Thank you, Dair," Frain whispered to me. He looked shaken. "How did you know?"

I pointed to my nose.

"The wolf caught their scent on the air, you say? Well, I am glad to have you with me. I wonder how much they would get for a crippled slave." He studied the trail with a sigh. "I suppose we must go off in the woods again. As long as we keep to a track we are easy prey for them or for robbers."

It was very true. But the going was slow in the woods. I missed my four sure paws, my narrow body that could glide between the branches. Frain was even slower than I.

Within a week after we landed, our provisions were low. There is a limit to how much food a human can carry, and we found it was not as much as was needed. The human body does not behave like the wolf body. It wants its food far more often, especially when it is on the move. So although our packs were lightening daily, our steps were heavier. There was not much forage in the forest. The wild grapevines which hung everywhere bore not even green fruit yet. We found a few mushrooms now and then which Frain ate. One day, after he had stripped the fungi off a rotting log, I turned it over and ate the grubs and earthworms I found underneath. When I had finished Frain handed me the mushrooms as well.

"My appetite has left me," he said wryly, and I felt worse than ever.

I smelled game everywhere, but I had no idea how to catch it. If I had been a wolf again I could have provided for us, I often thought. . . . Frain must have had some human notion of hunting, but he would not or could not use it. He threw stones that missed, set snares that were clumsy and caught nothing. I suspected that he could do better—how would he have survived, otherwise? But I had no way of saying so. I think he was afraid of killing anything, afraid of what the flow of blood might release in him.

We trudged on. We avoided slavers again, then robbers. Sometime in the second week we came to a burned place where the sun beat down on a dry meadow surrounded by the brushy forest. Tiny wild strawberries grew in the grass around the blackened stumps. We both picked them and ate them ravenously until our mouths and fingers were stained red. Frain ate more slowly than I because of his withered arm. He could only pluck one berry for my two. After a while I left the rest of them to him and tried to catch grasshoppers for myself in the taller weeds. It was hard, for the hands were stupid. I probably would have done better with my gaping mouth. But I caught a few and gulped them down. Frain looked at me oddly.

"This is laughable," he said. "We are starving faster than we can eat. Let us go on."

We walked until nightfall and then camped. There was no fire, for we did not dare make one. We ate our last scraps of hard shipsbread and then lay down to sleep. Frain drowsed off promptly—hunger made him tired. But I felt very restless, even more restless than usual, and the moon was at the full. I could see quite plainly Frain's face beside me, too thin. My bond brother, how was I to help him? . . . I got up finally and moved off to the crest of the nearest ridge, snuffed the night air, smelled deer not too far away and rabbits everywhere, and we were likely to die of want in the midst of it all. . . . I could not speak, but I could sing—that is to say, I could howl. I flung up my head and howled out my sorrow to my mother moon.

Some time later I walked softly back to camp. Frain was wide awake—I dare say my noise had roused him. As I approached his eyes fastened on me in startled fear. He jumped up and reached for his staff.

It's only me, I said, a woof. I stepped out of the brush so he could see me fully. He gave a long breath of relief and lay back down.

"Your eyes," he said, "they shine bright green in the moonlight, and you move so silently—I thought you were a panther."

The wild thing was on the prowl in me. I sensed it as surely as he did. I went to him and touched him lightly on the face—the first time I had done that, and he accepted it from me. Then I turned and left him, knowing quite surely and against all reason what I had to do for him. I had thought that my human form would be mine for life, but now I thought differently. . . .

Before I had taken a dozen strides into the dark I went down on all fours, and in a moment I was a wolf again, and I whined and barked aloud with the joy of it. From a standing start I leaped away, rushed into the thicket of night, ran down a rabbit almost before I knew it was there. *I beg your pardon, little sister, but I am famished,* I gasped, and I ripped it up on the spot, bolted down the warm, sustaining meat, food and drink in one, so good! Then I thought of Frain and I was ashamed. I had eaten and had saved nothing for him. I would kill him a deer, I thought, all by myself. No, I would not be able to drag such a large carcass back to him. . . . I found the rabbit's nest and absently bit down the little morsels it contained. I would have to find something I could take back to Frain.

It was dawn by the time I returned to him, trotting along with a large hare in my mouth. Frain was awake,

sitting and looking worried, waiting for me. I bounded
up to him and laid the hare at his feet, and for a moment
he looked as if he might faint. I had not considered how
my new form would shock him, and I cringed in apology.

"Dair?" he whispered.

I swung my head up and down in an exaggerated nod.

"Well. You make a lovely wolf." He blinked and
swallowed, recovering. He touched the hare. "Thank you.
But how am I to cook it? All sorts of riffraff will see the
smoke and come for breakfast."

I stood up, stretching, rippling my muscles, and gave
him a meaningful look. He laughed a low laugh.

"Just let them try, you say? All right, Dair."

He cooked and ate, and as it turned out no one disturbed us. By the time he was done morning was half
spent, so we made short miles that day. But I caught him a
coney for his supper, and I could see the strength returning to him. It made me glad. I felled a wild pig near our
camp that night and feasted and showed him the carcass
in the morning so that he could roast himself a haunch.

We journeyed on. I kept to my wolf form, worrying fitfully that I might not be able to find my way out of it
again but knowing in a deeper way that I would make a
change when it was time. After several days we found
ourselves in a slightly more settled country. Homesteads
lay widely scattered between woodlots and overgrown
meadows. I hoped Frain would ask some human for news
of Maeve, for I had heard nothing of a haunt in the forest
talk. It must have been because animals do not fear such
things the way people do—I could not suggest a sortie to
Frain, of course. I could scarcely tell him anything at all.

He did his scouting on his own. The day after I killed
a young deer he disappeared into a cottage with a slab
of the venison. I waited in a thicket for him, and pres-
ently he returned to me with bread, blackberries, cheese
and news.

"The south road to Jabul runs only a few days from
here," he reported. "Once we find it, we should be able
to follow it north to the place Trevyn named." He walked
on cheerfully.

But there was to be no walking in the days that followed. During the night, as bad luck would have it, Frain
became ill. Some strange human ailment—something in
the food had affected him. Pain bent him in knots, terrible
pain, and by morning he was out of his mind, whether

from the cramps or fever or fatigue I was not certain. He lay panting and did not recognize me when I sat beside him.

"Why, hello, Father," he said with a grim heartiness that chilled me.

I stared. Soon he reached up and touched my fur and laughed, a strained, unhealthy laugh.

"Fabron, the dog-king of Vaire! Scion of staghounds." Grasping my neck, he pulled himself up, sitting and feeling at the points of my ears. He frowned in puzzlement, trying to smooth them down to lie flat as a staghound's ought. "No, no, you are a usurper, I keep forgetting," he murmured. "You will die for that someday, Father, you know you will. Destiny—"

I whined in inquiry, and he lay back and wagged a finger at me, gravely reproachful.

"This taking of thrones, Fabron, greed for power and lust for gold and sell—sell—selling of your own child, you will die! Die! The hounds of hell rend you—" He sobbed, then struggled upright in rage. "Never mind!" he shouted wildly. "You're a dog anyway, and a son of a bitch, and that makes me a dog too, a pup, Shamarra said so—"

Silence took hold of him and he stood half bent over, staring fearfully. I went to him and pressed against his unsteady knees, trying to support and comfort him, but he did not notice. He was seeing things that were not there.

"Hands," he hissed, "hands of doom," and he inched back, taut. "Damn—lake," he panted. "Hates—me. The—face!"

He turned, stumbling, and tried to run, but pain staggered him and he fell—I bore the brunt of it, making a cushion for him until I scrambled out from under his thrashing weight. He was still running, legs beating the air madly, going nowhere, in the sort of fit that puppies suffer sometimes when they are about to die. Frightened, I tried to make him stop by lying on him, but he pummeled me with his one good hand, shouting, and drove me away. At last exhaustion quieted him and he lay in the dirt, covered with the leaf mold he had kicked up, panting again.

I went to fetch water—I in my wolf form, too dismayed and too unpracticed to find my way out of it—taking the flask in my mouth and finding a stream and dropping it in until it was full, padding back with it, spilling it over him. Again and again I did that until he was lucid enough to

53

grasp it and drink. Then with my teeth I tugged blankets over him, and he dozed.

Before midday he awoke again and lay gazing fixedly at a straight and slender gray-barked sapling that stood near-by.

"Shamarra," he addressed it, "I have never been able to understand what he did to you. How he could make that mystic tool into a hurtful, thrusting thing, a weapon of his hatred, no better than a broomstick—"

The thought seemed to both inflame and alarm him. He started struggling and shouting again. "I know what I would do to him if I were you, Shamarra! I would wind his guts around a stake. I would flay him alive. I would—no, oh, no—"

He started clawing at himself, his chest. Coming closer, I saw that his skin had gone as red as if it had been seared.

"Shamarra, not me!" he shouted fiercely. "Hag, why do you despise me? You know I am doomed to—oh, Tirell, my brother. . . ." He started to weep. He was raising great welts and bloody gashes on his body, tearing at himself, and I took his wrist in my jaws, struggling with him and trying to calm him. I knew now what ailed him, and I felt a cold chill thinking of it. The rye plague, the holy fire. Seed of it had come to him in the bread. Very likely it would leave him either insane or dead.

"Shamarra, please!" he groaned. "Let go!"

I could have cried for despair. But slowly, after some moments, a sense of hope came to me, for little as he seemed to know me he was speaking to me still in the language I understood, the Traderstongue. It must have become second nature to him in all the years of wandering. And how could he feel, I wondered, speaking always that mongrel tongue, a thing of mismatched parts and fragments as he himself—

"Let me die and have it over with," he whispered.

I suppose if it had not been for that matter of bathing in a forbidden lake he might have died. He was grievously ill for some days, unable to eat. At first he ranted and flailed, and I had to try to control him—luckily he had only the one arm and I was able to keep him from hurting himself too much. Later the fire left his skin but he lay like a corpse, nearly senseless, wasting away until his fair skin was stretched taut over the bones of his face and they showed through whitely. Once again I felt that I was failing him, I in my wolf form. I brought him meat, but it was

54

of no use to him. All I could do was lick his face and lie close beside him. The warmth of my furry body seemed to ease the pain in his belly. In the night he would stir and moan and whisper of Tirell and Shamarra and Fabron the doomed dog his father until I pressed my muzzle against his face, and then he would throw his arm around my neck, hug me and sleep for a little while.

I knew I should wish for my human form again and nurse him properly, but I could not. Wishes are like dreams—they will not be directed. Without true desire I could not make the change, and I felt sure that Frain would never have put his arm around Dair the man or let me warm and comfort him in the night. Guiltily, foolishly, I kept bringing him meat and the touch of warm fur, until one morning after a restless night he turned his head and looked at me.

"Dair," he murmured.

I sat up, ears pricked at attention, scarcely daring to breathe.

"What . . . I have been sick."

I nodded.

"I—how long?"

I had lost count of the days, but with a forepaw I made many scratches in the dirt. Frain gazed back at me in amazement.

"But I do not remember anything," he said softly, and I think my eyes narrowed somewhat as I looked back at him. For perhaps he could not remember, did not want to remember the things he had seen and the things he had said, but I felt certain that a part of him had always been aware, like the watcher in a dream, the one who whispers in the ear of the mind, "this is a dream," even as the mind is screaming. I felt sure he would not have been awake and speaking to me if it were not so. For the first time then I guessed at the hidden strength of Frain. And I guessed as well that the hidden fears, the darkness he did not want to face, lay closer at hand than he was willing to admit.

Chapter Seven

All his strength of body had left him. He could scarcely stand or walk. Nevertheless, with my help, he crawled to the wood I had gathered for him and made himself a fire, and he managed in a crude fashion to boil meat for broth. He lapsed into a sitting stupor while it was cooking, but as soon as it was ready I roused him, and after it had cooled he drank it down. He nibbled at shreds of the meat, and then he slept, quite soundly.

For several days thereafter he ate as often as he was able, a little at a time. I brought him every sort of food that I could forage. As I saw that he would be well, and as my fear for him lessened somewhat, I became moody and fearful on my own account, though I felt I should be glad. Sense of failure was strong in me—I had been so long a wolf, I wondered if I would ever again make a human companion for him. If only we had reached my mother's abode, perhaps she would have been able to help me. . . . I became impatient with the slowness of Frain's healing. My muddle of feeling came to a head one evening as I studied the flames of the campfire, restless and ashamed by turns, and fervently eager to have the journey over with—Maeve's home lay only a few days' travel away. I wished we had a horse for Frain to ride. I wished that I could carry him myself. He was so helpless still— I pictured him lying hacked by robbers. Unease and the image moved me to a woeful howl.

Frain was startled. "Dair, whatever is the matter?" he asked. Then he walked over to me unsteadily and caressed me, patting my head and the thick fur of my neck. "Everything will be all right," he assured me.

56

Feeling foolish and abashed, I skulked off to hunt myself some supper. Later, when I came back to camp, he was asleep. I lay beside him and dozed, and in my doze I dreamed of the horse. It was strong and slate gray, and in the dream I wanted to be that horse, to carry Frain swiftly to Maeve and safety. I would never have thought of it in daylight, I had never considered that I could be anything except a wolf and a man. But the dream bore me up. . . . My paws were hooves, my body a massive thing on absurdly thin legs, my neck lithe and long. I snorted and awoke myself to discover that I had strayed some distance from Frain. I was the gray horse, and I was eating twigs. The green taste of them shocked me more than anything else about the change. I had never been fond of greens.

Well, I told myself, it is only for a few days. I hoped that was so.

When Frain awoke in the morning, his eyes lit on me with a look of startled joy and he came gently over and caught me by the forelock. "Good horse," he whispered. "I am glad you are amenable." Then he called, "Dair!" and looked all around him eagerly.

This was a problem—he did not recognize me. I nudged him in the ribs with my sizable nose.

"Oof!" he protested. "Dair! Come see this!" he called more loudly, beginning to look worried. I did not often leave him for long or roam far away for fear that slavers or something might harm him. "Where the bloody flood can he have got to?" Frain muttered.

I could not change back to wolf or man again to show him. At least I did not think I could without losing the horse.

"Dair!" he shouted, forgetting all caution.

Here I am! I growled, butting him hard with my head. I am sure he had never heard a horse growl before. He whirled and let go of my forelock, stepping back to stare at me.

"Dair?" he whispered.

I nodded hugely. But horses nod for any number of reasons, including flies, and Frain looked doubtful.

"If you are really Dair," he said, "paw with your right front hoof three times."

I did it promptly. I was not proud when it came to pleasing him.

"Now the left, twice," he ordered.

He still did not believe me! I pawed hard, annoyed. I laid back my ears at him and rolled my eyes. Frain stared at me a moment longer, then began to laugh, loudly and a bit wildly. "Dair, a horse!" he whooped. "I must be losing my mind—well, why not? You make a ridiculous horse. Your mane is nothing but bristles and your hair sticks out in all directions as if it is trying to be fur."

I reared back and wheeled away from him, affronted. He came after me at once, still snickering but contrite. "Dair, don't be angry," he soothed. "I'm sorry—I am just surprised, that is all—here I stand, apologizing to a horse!" A fresh fit of merriment swept him up, but he sobered at once when I snorted at him. "And full of humble gratitude," he added. "Please don't be angry. I'll get my things ready at once."

He hastily broke camp. He placed one blanket on me, folded, by way of saddle, and put the other over my rump with the packs slung on top of it. "How am I to mount you?" he asked, still with mirth in his voice. "I am as weak as a newborn pup."

We managed it with the aid of a stump. I bowed to my foreknees to receive him. Then I straightened, and he laid his head on my neck as we worked our way through the trees. All my anger left me at that touch. I went as softly as I could, trying not to jostle him. As soon as we reached an open space I eased into a trot, as wolflike a trot as I could make it.

"Such gaits!" Frain marveled from my back. "It is like riding smooth water, sitting on a gray cloud. Even the packs lie steady. Dair, you wonder, you make a superb horse. I am so sorry I laughed at you."

He had been laughing at himself or at fate, I saw that now. I trotted on contentedly. Being a horse was not nearly as satisfactory as being a wolf—horses think of uncouth things, rivalry and grazing and sore hocks and submission and mares, and I felt all the nervousness of the prey, the grass-eater, I who liked meat—still, there was the power of my massive body to be enjoyed. I wanted to spook, to fling up my head and run, but I knew Frain would not have been able to deal with that. He was still very weak.

When we camped at dusk I was pleased by the journey we had come. Frain did not have much to eat, but he seemed hopeful. I grazed distastefully. Horses are like humans, they need always to be filling their bellies. . . . I hoped I would not be eating grass for long. And indeed, the next day before noon we found the road that snakes up from Jabul. It was only a gravel track, really. We turned left on it, northward. By nightfall, I thought excitedly, we might be at my mother's dwelling, at Maeve's house in the haunt.

I sped along eagerly with Frain nearly asleep on my back. We were careless, both of us. We should have known we would meet robbers on this main road. And I was a horse, yet! They wanted me.

They were quite close before I scented them. I snorted to warn Frain and sprang into a gallop, hoping to run past them before they could attack us. But I felt Frain losing his seat. The proud fool, why would he not hang on by my mane? I had to slow down. The robbers blocked the road, six burly men of them with weapons. I wanted to rear and attack them with my forehooves, but I was afraid of throwing Frain. I could do nothing. One of them grasped me by the forelock, and two of them dragged Frain from my back. He had his knife out—that was why he had not clung to me. He struck at them. But they were used to knives and in no awe of a one-armed man, and perhaps his effort was not of the best—they laughed at him. Laughed, at Frain!

Fear left me. With sudden, stormy force rage rushed through me instead. In an instant I was a wolf, and I turned on the man who held me and sheared off his hand above the wrist with one snap of my powerful jaws. The outlaws fled, screaming. My eerie change alone probably would have been enough to unnerve them, but in fact I was huge—as big as the horse, Frain told me later, whether from wrath or from haste in the changing. I bounded after my human prey, caught up with them in a single leap, slashing at their rumps and snarling as if they were so many deer.

"Dair!"

It was Frain. I stopped at once and let the robbers run off, turned to see him standing in the pathway and looking down at an outlaw's severed hand, his face ashen. One glance at him and I was myself again in human form at last—I could not have been otherwise.

"That does not help as much as you might think," he said as if I had done it on purpose to reassure him. "There's blood on your mouth, Dair."

That which is honorable in the wolf is less so in the man. I winced and turned away, trying to cleanse myself with my hands. All that happened was that the blood got on them, too. . . . Frain limped over to me, sticking his knife in his belt, walking shakily.

"Never mind," he said. "You were magnificent."

We had better get away from here, I said.

I fetched our packs and we strode off at the best pace Frain could muster. The track soon turned to a trail and wound its way up a slope. I saw tall pines rising ahead.

We're almost there! I exclaimed. Frain probably heard it as an excited whimper.

In another moment I sensed the haunt. I felt it as a heaviness in the air, a slight chill. Trevyn had told me about haunts. The souls whose silent presence I sensed were those whose passions bound them to earth, who for whatever reason could not fly. But passion itself was purged from them by death, and they in themselves were nothing, only formless reflections—

Frain stopped where he stood with a gasp of terror, and I saw the fear-sweat running on him like rainwater.

"What is it, what thing is here?" he cried wildly. "I cannot go in there, I can't go on!"

Why did the bodiless shades undo men so? Trevyn had told me about the panic fear, the blind eyes, the madly running legs. He had not thought that I would feel it, as indeed I did not. But Frain dropped his pack and turned back the way we had come. He stopped before I had to catch hold of him. Twenty paces behind us four of the robbers had gathered, whispering to each other and pointing at us.

"Great Adalis," Frain groaned.

They would not come any closer to the haunt. And within it was safety. If only I could tell Frain that! I could have seized him and carried him in, he was so light and frail by then, but I was afraid he would hate me for it. I wanted him to welcome my touch someday.

Come on, I urged him—a whine.

He trembled. He looked at the brigands and at me. Then with a wild cry of despair or defiance he turned and ran into the pine forest and the haunt.

He lurched from side to side as he ran, staggering and struggling. He always ran awkwardly, leaning to one side because of his withered arm, but this was a struggle of a different sort. It wrenched my heart to look at him. He was in pain, he seemed scarcely able to breathe. Yet he kept on. I followed close after him, not daring to touch him. Up the steep, winding path we went, with Frain panting all the way and letting out gasping, grunting sounds, strangling sounds, animal sounds. . . . Tall trees closed around us and our enemies were shut from sight. Then Frain fell.

It was not that he stumbled or fainted. It was more as if he had been knocked down, stunned by a powerful, unseen blow. He lay with lidded eyes and a face gone corpse white, his back arched with the effort to rise, every muscle taut. He clawed his way a few inches forward. He still needed to fight, to struggle onward. . . . I grasped him under the shoulders and pulled him upright, supporting him but letting him stand. Once again he staggered forward with the blind courage of a hurt thing.

I could see a rooftop ahead.

Just a few more steps, I told Frain, though of course he could not understand me. *Just a few more steps—*

The chill left the air. Warmth of welcome was all around us—we had come within the charmed circle, and the spirits were our friends and strong protectors, our bulwark against any harm. The forest ended as well and we stood at the edge of a clearing. Frain felt the change. He opened his eyes and sobbed once, then nearly toppled. I put both arms around him, trying to steady him.

"Dair. . . ."

He laid his head on my shoulder and wept. In all we had been through I had never seen him weep so. I held him as best I could, patted at him, tried to comfort him, making useless, throaty sounds. I could have wept myself.

"I have seen that face again," he choked, "and it is hideous, hideous!"

It was as Trevyn had said. He was far braver than we could know or understand, for what he faced was fearsome. After a while he quieted, leaning against me, accepting my concern, my clumsy attentions and my love. Finally he straightened, the tears still streaking his face. He raised his head to meet my eyes. He reached up to touch my brow. He had never done that.

"Dair," he said, "thank you, ten thousand times thank you. I owe you more than I can say. I have never had such a friend."

I wanted to fall at his feet in my gratitude. But he needed me beside him just then—and as he spoke my mother came out to greet us both.

61

INTERLUDE I
from The Book of Suns

Now it is said that fire and water are elements that exclude one another, that never meet. But I tell you, People of Peace, that in the One all things meet, and I will tell you a tale of a thing the One has done.

It is said also that the sun is a great golden man, or a stallion, or a chariot or a fiery wheel. All these things may be true. But I tell you the sun is a great golden swan. By day it flies, and by dawning and dusk it floats on the surrounding ocean, and by night it dives deep, for it must swim the dark flood that lies beneath. Arrowswift, arrowstraight it swims from the west unto the east where it rises to fly again. And the sunswan is made of fire, but the flood does not quench it.

And it is said yet once again that the moon is a swan as well, a silver swan that floats on a river of stars. And so indeed it is. But it is true as well that the moon is a comely woman, and a jewel, and a pearly ship, and a white deer, a hart. And the moonswan is made of white fire.

Now in those Beginning days moonswan and sunswan were one. For the One lived in perfection then, encompassing all things, male and female and all their passions, all loves and hates. White fire and bright, day and night were One. There was no rift then, no shattering of essence into multiplicity. But where there is life there must be movement, and the movement circled and quickened until it gathered itself into a tide and surge which broke the surface of that entity. And that which was moon burst free, sundered from the other part, and ran as a white hart across the heavens. And the sun pursued it as a lost love.

Up, ever upward to the navel of heaven they ran, golden stag and white hart. And down into the deep they dove, golden swan and argent, and swam full circle, and up streaming into the high heaven again they flew. And when moon found it could not outstrip the sun, the white hart turned and pierced him with its sharp horns, and the sunswan fell spiraling down and down until it fell to rest on a high and hidden place of earth. I am torn, swan cried, torn self from self. My own flesh and form has betrayed me.

The wound was not mortal, but blood ran out of it and stained some fiery feathers red. Sunswan moistened them further with tears, for he felt doom and all the strife and sorrow of mortality in his wound and in a new thing that was coming over earth, a strange dark presence called night. And moon had sworn that thenceforth she would ever be at opposite reach of earth from him, night-swan to his day, dusk to his dawn. So the sun wept. But as he did so he set about to make something, a marvel that would in end time bring her back to him.

With his great bill he plucked the feathers from his wounded breast, feathers of fire. And that fire was wet with blood and with dew of his tears and with salt water of the flood. Such petals as never were he fashioned there, petals made of flamefeather and water of the flood. With them he made a flower like no other flower that has ever been seen, his own child born of his flesh and of the conflicting elements, as alive as he was. He washed it in the pure waters of that place, waters that welled from the navel of earth itself, and it blazed ever brighter.

Now, he said, you will serve to purify with fire the one who will come to find you. And you will confer on that mortal the power to bring all things back to One. And may that day come soon.

He taught the flower to hide in earth until the time had come. But that day did not come soon, and it has not come yet, nor will it come until the dawning of the days of the final age, when the tide has turned back to primal truth. And still the flower hides. It comes forth only in the dark night of that one day a year when its parent sun is in his fullest bloom and power.

Now you ask me, who is this one who will come? A hero of greatest stature, you are thinking, perhaps one of the Sun Kings who have been promised to you. For the final age is drawing near, and you can feel that. But I tell you, Fair Folk, my first children, this passing will not take place as you expect. He who plucks the fire flower shall not be the strongest one, but the one who needs it the most. And a scion of the Sun Kings shall aid him.

book two
MAEVE

Chapter One

I am Maeve, mortal woman, soul now, speaking to you from the stardark realm. I was Moon Mother when I lived; she lived in me, as she has in many others. She, an aspect of Alys All-Mother who is at one with the ineffable One. . . . Fertility was my function. Trevyn was Very King, even though he was hardly more than a boy when I knew him, so I went to him and conceived Dair— I went to him the seven nights of the swelling moon. Then when he brought the magic back to Isle I was there, I was a wolf that worships the moon, and I bore him a lupine son.

I was rather expecting that Dair would come to me, but I was not at all expecting Frain.

Old Dorcas, my servant, brought the news to me that strangers were standing in the meadow. She came running into the room where I was at work packing some things for my journey—more about that later. She was very excited and rather afraid, for strangers came seldom. So I went on out and there was Dair, buck naked and beautiful. I suppose I ought to say that I was a matronly sort, my body thick, my clothing drab, my hair pulled back in a bun and streaked with gray; I am sure I surprised Trevyn very much by giving him his son. But I have always known beauty when I see it, and my son was supremely beautiful. I knew him not only by that but by his amethyst eyes. I hurried to him and embraced him.

Mother! he exclaimed, returning the embrace. It was only a growl, but I understood him well enough.

"What makes you think I am your mother?" I teased.

Your eyes—they are the color of violets in shadow.

66

"Yes." I hugged him and let him go. "Who is this other one?" I asked.

Frain. The tone said "Friend." The fellow stood by Dair's side, pale and plainly shaken. He was a winsome youth with auburn hair and an earnest, searching look; it was not until later that I noticed the crippled arm. I extended my hand to him, speaking to him in Traderstongue, for I could see he was a foreigner. There were no redheads in Tokar except slaves.

"You are very welcome here," I told him, pressing his damp and trembling palm. "Let us go in and have some tea."

Dorcas had the kettle on, for a wonder. It was mint tea, quite strong; it brought tears to the eyes. Dair and I talked all in a warm rush, remembering each other, remembering Trevyn; how was he, his wife, his child? And Isle— Frain sat and sipped his tea and listened to us. Gradually his tight shoulders relaxed and the color came back into his face.

"I wish I could talk to Dair like that," he said to me.

We had been speaking the Old Language, of course, and Frain was not one of the special few who remember it. I shook my head regretfully.

"The Elder Tongue was born in me and in Trevyn," I told him. "It is not a language that can be learned or taught. Unless . . ." I let the thought drift away. It was not yet time to speak of quests and journeys. At that moment the plain, close kitchen, the low dusty rafters and wooden table that I had been so willing to leave seemed to me the dearest things in my life. Home. For thirty years this squat little house had been my home.

"He is so much wiser than I am," Frain said. "He senses danger and runs boldly in the dark, while I blunder into peril and shy from mere phantoms. . . . What was it that frightened me so? I had to be led in here like a child by the wild man." He gave Dair an affectionate glance.

"Shadows," I said. "Shades of the dead. Not a hero in ten thousand could have come in here. You are a rare one, Frain."

"But I had not thought I was afraid of the dead," he protested. "I have met them before. In Vale, souls fly up as birds. The Luoni harry them to deprive them of their afterlife. Then they must dive and swim—"

"So what is there to be frightened of?" I asked.

"A lot! People in my country are afraid of anything

that flies, of the night, the screams of the Luoni, and they are afraid of flowing water. They say the rivers have boneless hands that will pull a person down. But I never saw them, and I was never afraid of noises in the night or birds or water until—until that last time." He stopped, suddenly pallid.

"Go on," I said. Fear has to be met.

"I looked into Shamarra's lake and I saw that face," he whispered.

Then he saw it again today! Dair put in excitedly. I waited, wanting Frain to say that for himself.

"Well, the shades are like the water, in a way," I remarked when he said nothing more. "They are fluid, formless, colorless. They themselves are practically nothing. Anything they cause you to see is a reflection."

Reflection of what? Frain should have asked. Perhaps he did ask himself and could not sit still for the answer. He got up, looking bleak, and I knew better than to pursue.

"Let me find you something to eat," I said.

"There's a little food in my pack yet," Frain muttered, "wherever I left it—oh, Eala, it's down beyond the trees."

"I'll get it," Dair offered, and he ambled out. Old Dorcas hid her face in modesty at the sight of him and fled to a secluded portion of the house.

We ate lunch when he returned. It was mostly green beans from the garden; Dair chewed them with much sour grimacing. Already I knew that he would be out on the hunt for meat after dark. I smiled and turned my attention to Frain.

"Tell me why you are here."

We talked through the afternoon. It took that long to get much sense out of him. I think that he himself did not really know what he wanted of me, so he had to tell me his whole story before I could understand the joke fate or his own foolhardiness had played on him. He had thought Isle to be Ogygia—well, he might have been not too far wrong. Isle was a magical place. He had spoken with Alys there. He had to find Shamarra, he told me, and the goddess had sent him to me for help.

I knew nothing of Shamarra, night birds or Vale either. "What exactly did she say?" I asked. I knew the riddling ways of the goddess.

"To go east."

"Did she say you would find Shamarra in the east?"

"No," he admitted. "She did not say where Shamarra was at all. She said you would help me."

"But did she say what I was to help you to do?"

He sighed. "Some nonsense about fern flower," he said, "and fire meeting flood."

I sat thinking of my own quest. The Source lay east, if I could judge by the remembered lore of the elves and the yearning that sang to me from the rising sun. I tried not to let my judgment be skewed by the tug that was on me. No—the truth was plain, tug or no tug.

"Shamarra is not your true quest," I said.

I saw his eyebrows leap up. He did not feel well enough acquainted with me to argue, but I knew he did not agree. And I knew just as surely that I would be taking him with me to the Source.

Dair meandered in. He had been out foraging, and he looked pleased with himself and with the world at large. He carried a basket full of mushrooms and blackberries, and he wore a sort of breechclout in deference to Dorcas's squeamishness. I remembered the days when Trevyn used to go about like that, and my heart swelled.

"Come here," I said to him. "I was just about to tell Frain that I am to go on a journey."

I noticed your bags. He came over and sat at the table with us. *When will you leave?*

"Not for several days. Not until you two have had a chance to rest. Frain does not look well."

He has been very ill.

"I wish I could understand you two," Frain sighed.

I switched to Traderstongue. It would be difficult to explain myself to him in such a clumsy tongue. It would have been difficult to explain my reasons in any language of man. I knew what I was doing or to do in one sense, a nighttime sense, a dream sense, but in the daytime sense I did not know in the least what I was about. I had a vague notion what Dair was for, and that was all.

"I have been seeing flowers made of red flame in the sunrise," I said tentatively, "and in the hearth, and I have been hearing voices in the night when I am half asleep, voices telling me it is time the old woman came out of her wood. I have sometimes thought that the One has been talking to me. I wish I were foolish enough to feel sure. At any rate, I have made up my mind. I must leave this place and set out to find the Source."

Frain merely nodded. It was nothing to him what I did.

He was not seeing the safe haven of thirty years left behind.

"And I feel quite certain, Frain, that you are to come with me."

He sat up at attention then. "Only if Shamarra might be there," he said.

Little did I know of Shamarra and her vengeful ways. "She might be there or anywhere," I declared, resorting to sophistry, certain that he would not respond to better truth. This birdwoman was the least pressing of his needs, I knew that by then, but she gave the only hold I had on him. I would bribe him into obedience by means of Shamarra.

"And if she is there how are you to recognize her?" I demanded. "And even if she were to sit on your hand in bird form, how would you speak to her? If you cannot understand Dair, you will not be able to understand a night bird."

His shoulders sagged. "The goddess said I would not be able to—well, help her," he mumbled. "But I have to keep on trying, don't you see? Because of—the way I am."

I stifled a sigh of exasperation.

"There is a song the elves used to sing—" I began.

"Elves?" he interrupted.

"The old folk, a fair, tall race. Those who went before." Did he know nothing? "They sailed to Elwestrand. None have set foot on the mainland for tens of thousands of years, but some of us still remember them and the Source whence they came, they and their bright stones." I stared down his doubt. "There is a song they used to sing, and it is in *Dol Solden*, too, I believe, the mystic Book of Suns. A song about the Source and the magical fern that grows there.

> Fern flower, fire flower,
> Burn, burn when the great tide turns.
> Fern flower, show your power.
> The Swan Lord will be there to see,
> To grasp the stem that burns
> And speak with thee,
>   learn melody,
>   and sing with wind and tree."

Dair sat looking at me in suppressed excitement, and Frain quite blankly.

"But it is nonsense," he protested. "Ferns don't have flowers."

"That is why this one is so singular," I said. "The legend is that the flower of this fern, if plucked at the proper time, will give the bearer power to understand almost anything—the speech of water and trees and wind and even stars." I took significant pause. "And, of course, birds."

"You mean Shamarra?" Frain jumped as if he had been jabbed. "But when is the proper time?"

"Midnight on Midsummer's Eve."

"But—is it far?" Midsummer was nearly upon us.

"Very far, I imagine. We might get there by this time next year."

"Another year!" he groaned.

"You have nearly infinite years before you," I reminded him gently. "And so has Shamarra."

That settled him. "What is this Source?" he inquired, with the first real, sensible interest he had shown. "The Source of what?"

"Of everything! All that is." I looked at him in surprise. "Does no one tell tales of the Source in your land, of the Beginning?"

"Of Adalis, of how she lay upon the flood and mothered forth all that is in Vale—"

"Well," I said rather too sharply, "you have seen that there is more to the world than Vale."

"Adalis is true goddess," he returned just as sharply. "I have seen that as well."

"She is in Aene." I smoothed the edge off my voice. Ignorant he might be, but he was courageous, and he was *there,* in my house, in the flesh—an exceptional event. There had to be some reason for it. And he was arching his brows again.

"The nameless One," I explained. I had used the elfin word; my mistake. "Aene is sun, moon, empty sky and all that is on earth. Aene is dawn and dusk. Aene sang the world into being. The Source is the place of that singing. Strong magic is there."

What else is there? Dair asked.

There was a quality about Dair that was too goodnatured to be called irreverence or flippancy; it was only that he was so very blunt. Frain sensed the tone of the question even though he could not apprehend the content, and he laughed out loud. I had to smile.

"Truly, I don't know," I said. "We shall have to see."

71

I think I have already seen that flower, Dair said, and I nodded at him.

"I have not yet said that I am coming," Frain put in.

"Ah, but you are," I told him. "What else could be intended for you?" I felt a comforting certainty grow in me. His presence, like Dair's, was a proof, a sign.

"I suppose I am," he admitted. "That is, if Dair—Dair?" He turned to his companion in sudden anxiety. "Dair, are you coming on this—errand?"

Of course.

Dair followed the reassurance with a nod, and Frain smiled and relaxed. I felt compunction take hold of me. Such children they were, really, and what was I leading them into?

"It will not be easy," I warned. "None of it will be easy, and the fern flower least of all. It is said to exact a fearsome price."

"Nothing in my life has been easy," Frain said.

Chapter Two

Five days later we set out with as little ado as possible, though there were some tears. I left the house in the care of old Dorcas and Jare, her husband, they who had been my servants for many years. When they died the place would go to ruin, but not before. It gave me some comfort that they would tend it awhile. For their part, they felt comforted that I went with companions at my side.

So off we trudged, toting heavy packs of bread, dried meat and the like. We walked eastward. We walked, for the most part, for the next several months, following nothing more than sunrise and my instinct and the gentle, insistent tug of the unseen Source. We walked out of sycamore forest and into oak and beech and beyond that into ilex and scrub pine. Our packs soon lightened as we ate up our provisions, and Dair took to keeping us supplied with meat, slipping in and out of his wolf form with ever increasing ease and skill. Frain watched him in wonder and in love.

"How do you do it, the shape changing?" he asked Dair as we sat by the fire one night. He had taken to talking to Dair with the aid of a translator—me. The conversations were awkward, especially since Dair was not by nature the talkative sort. But Frain persevered. There was a dogged quality about Frain.

I don't know, said Dair. True enough; he never spoke less than truth. He was an instinctive being, a child of the wilderness.

"You must know something," said Frain. "How did it happen to you the first time?"

I—it was you. I wanted to befriend you. I wanted it so badly I howled.

Frain looked both startled and pensive, remembering something. "I believe it was the same the second time, and the third," he mused. "Desire—"

"More is needed than mere desire," I told both of them. I was a shape changer too; just let them wait and see! "It is a matter of being with whatever is. Of being no longer separate. Being at one."

"What?" said Frain, for he was so human, so set apart that he was not even aware of it. And Dair growled in equal puzzlement, for he was so much a part of whatever he sensed. . . . I stared at him.

"There is a risk, too," I said slowly, "of losing self to instinct, the fate of the form. But there can be no changing without risk of loss."

Frain sat folded in upon himself, looking lonesome. I felt sure that Dair had never comprehended that peculiar human quality of being at odds with the world, that cosmic loneliness. But he was soon to learn the meaning of it.

I will never forget the night we first heard the cry of the wild wolves.

There must have been famine in the north that had driven them to the southern woods. Mournful hunger was in their voices. We heard them at dusk as we ate our cold meat, and I for one felt a sudden urge to make a campfire, though we needed none for cooking. Frain glanced at me askance, his face taut.

"Will they bother us, do you think?" he asked, keeping his voice low.

Game was not scarce, so I judged that men—robbers— would be the greater danger. We made no fire. We sat in the gathering darkness, listening to the voices of the wolves, silvery voices that summoned their fellows to the hunt, harmonious and very beautiful.

They ring through me like harp song, said Dair suddenly. I glanced at him sharply. His eyes were glimmering, shining greenly, not with joy but with yearning and a sort of lust.

"What is it?" Frain asked me, alerted by something in the tone of Dair's utterance.

"I think he would like to join the hunt."

Wolf notes were reaching a wild chorus. *Like!* Dair exclaimed, panting with feeling. *It is hardly the word. I*

74

could die with longing. The musky creature smells, and that green darkness—there are no words for what I feel.

It was true, there were none, not even in the Old Language that cannot tell false. But I knew the pang, for I had felt it myself. Wilderness call—one might as well be in thrall. I tried to hide my sympathy, watching him narrowly. He sat trembling, his hands twitching like restless paws, his nostrils pulsating, temples pulsating with the force of the blood that raced through the veins of his bare neck.

Frain watched him as well, his brown eyes troubled. "Did you never run with the wolves in Isle, Dair?" he asked, quite gently.

Dair shook his head violently. *No. I heard them, but never so close, so calling, and I was younger—*

"He has no business with them," I snapped. "Dair, don't you know you are meant for something more than running with a pack?"

He didn't answer me. Even as I spoke his wolf form came on him all in a rush like loveheat, of its own accord. He stretched his muzzle skyward and howled; the sound shivered through the air. The chorus of the wild wolves abruptly ceased, and Frain's cry of shock sounded painfully loud in the dusky silence.

"Dair! Wait!"

Dair ran to him and laid his long head in his lap with a whine, a wordless appeal. Frain held tightly to the taut, quivering body.

"He has to go," I said, my tone peevish to hide bothersome emotion. "He has to—find out. . . ."

Fate can be a heartless thing.

"He says he will come back to you."

Frain swallowed and loosened his grasp. "Go," he said, and Dair bounded off into the dark forest.

We listened awhile. The wolfsong had begun again. It moved farther away.

"No harm is likely to come to him, is it, Maeve?" Frain asked me when he finally spoke. I hastened to reassure him.

"Harm, to Dair? What harm could come to him from wolves? He is a wolf himself."

"He will be back," Frain muttered, to himself rather than to me. "He said he would."

Why, then, if all was well, were we both sitting anxiously in the night?

Neither of us slept, although I sometimes pretended to. At the first light of dawn Frain was up and pacing. From time to time faint howls sounded far to the east. Dair did not return.

"Something has happened," Frain declared with fanatical certainty a scant hour after sunrise. "I must go find him."

"You cannot find him," I said.

"The pack last howled eastward." He pointed.

"He will not be with the pack. Stay here. You will lose your way in the forest if you go off, and then he will have to find *you*."

Frain glared at me, insulted, but worry won out over injured pride. "Dair needs my help. I am sure of it," he said, and started away. I caught hold of him.

"Stay," I said angrily. "It is bad enough that one of you two infants is out on his own."

He shook off my hand.

"Stay and give Dair a chance to keep his word," I said in a different tone, reaching through anger to truth. Frain stared at me, then nodded.

He kept to camp, but restively. Neither of us ate. We stood erect and alert all that long morning, as if any moment something might pounce on us with teeth and claws and send us reeling into disaster.

Dair told us later what had happened.

The wolves, the wild pack, his brothers. They had struck a fine stag that led them a long, swift chase. Dair followed the sound and scent through the night, feeling the surge of his own power and grace. He heard the brief triumph howl at the kill, but it was daybreak before he found them where they lay feasting.

Seven of them in the sunlight—

He spoke in wonder of the colors of their pelages. Two were tawny fawn, one cinnamon, one nearly red, one brown, one gray and one, the largest and the leader, pure black. That one was as large as he. But he did not get to look at them for long; they scented him almost as soon as he sighted them. *Man!* they barked, and with that warning they streaked away, leaving their kill.

I must have lost my mind, Dair said wryly. *I ran after them.*

And he caught up with them in a few moments, for he was swift and long of limb. He sped into their midst, and of course they were terrified by his strangeness, appearance

76

and essence that did not match. Their terror made them savage. They attacked him fiercely.

His thick fur gave him some protection. But he could not stand against them all, and within the minute he was forced to flee, limping and bleeding from a dozen slashes. They pursued him. He could no longer outrun them, wounded as he was, and they harried him. He ran at first back toward our camp, but as they continued to follow, biting and snarling and worrying at him, he thought hazily that he might be bringing danger down upon us and he changed direction, setting a twisting course through the ilex trees. After a while, sluggish from full bellies, the pack circled away and left him. Dair struggled on, no longer sure of his bearings, feeling lost and desperate to find us. He would not stop to rest or lick his wounds until he had rejoined us.

Maybe the wolf god knows the effort it cost him—he endured. He came back to us. About noon of the next day he staggered back to the campsite where Frain and I stood frantically disputing. One of his eyes was swollen shut from a cut just above it, and the ear on that side was torn, and his gray fur was all dappled and clotted with brownish red—he had one glimpse of Frain's shocked and anguished face and he was himself again in human form. His injuries looked even worse on his furless human skin.

"Oh, no!" Frain cried out, choking. "Dair—"

He stood swaying a moment, and then he fell against Frain, who caught him with his one good arm and laid him down. But Dair came to himself again in a moment. He had needed that human embrace, I think.

I am sorry, he muttered thickly.

"Hush," said Frain fiercely, almost as if he could understand him. "Maeve, water. Eala, if only I could help him—"

We used all our water on him. There was not enough to properly cleanse the wounds. We concentrated on the ones around his face and head, binding them as neatly as we were able, hoping they would not scar too badly.

"We ought to sear the rest for safety," I said, trying to keep my voice steady. Searing is an ugly business. Frain had Dair's head on his lap at the time, and he clutched at him protectively.

"He won't sicken! He's as strong as a bear."

Do it, Dair said. *I don't care.* There were tears in his

voice, and not because of physical pain, either. I felt sure of it. Frain and I both stared at him.

"Don't try to be noble, Dair," I snapped. But I took him at his word and prepared for the searing, made the fire and placed a blade in it to heat. I found myself being very stern. Only toughness would see me through this. When the knife was ready I took it and advanced on Dair, my face hard.

"Must this be done?" Frain appealed.

"Yes. Burns are horrible, Frain, but contagion is worse. I've seen—" I did not say what I had seen. A shudder of foreboding passed through me, taking my breath for a moment. I closed my eyes, but I could not trace it.

"Go find us water," I said to Frain.

"I am not entirely a weakling, Maeve," he retorted coldly. Pride. And I had only been trying to spare him. . . . He stayed where he was and took Dair's hands in his one.

"All right," I said, knelt and applied the blade.

Dair bore it as an animal might, shaking and wincing but not crying out. Silent tears ran down his face. The leg wounds were the worst, but we cauterized all of them over the course of the next hour except the cuts on his face. They were not very large, and we hoped they would not fester or scar. Dair clung to Frain throughout it all. I could see how he needed the comfort of his presence, so it was I who went for water finally, a long walk, and by the time I got back dusk was coming on and Dair had lapsed into an exhausted sleep. Frain and I eased him into the softest bed we could make him. Then we sat and tried to eat, but neither of us could eat much.

"You said he would not be hurt," Frain muttered, staring at me fixedly, as if I had betrayed him.

"I was wrong," I said. Truth. I had thought Dair would be forced to make a choice. Instead, it had been made for him, and quite harshly.

"He had to go, nevertheless," I added. "He had to face his fate sometime."

Frain only looked away from me, shrugging. He would not admit his own anger at me, and for once I was not willing to press him. I felt worn out.

We watched over Dair by turns that night, but he did not need us. I was expecting fever, but none came. The next day he was in pain, but he made light of it. He ate some meat, and on toward evening he told us his story.

"And I thought you had more sense," I grumbled at him, still being stern.

I am ashamed, he murmured, making me sorry for my words.

"Why?" I scoffed. "We are all fools one time or another."

For—leaving Frain. . . .

Of course his shame did not extend to me—mere mothers do not usually merit such concern. Sighing, I turned to Frain and told him what Dair had said, not really expecting much help from him. I had not yet learned to know him well, to realize that he had a habit of exceeding expectations.

"But I know that call that sings in the wind," he said promptly to Dair. His smile was warm, not forgiving but better yet—there was no need for forgiveness, that smile said. I gaped at Frain in astonishment. I had not known such understanding was in him.

"I heard it when I stood on my first mountaintop," he said, his face and the look in his eyes vital, alive with the memory. "I remember the marvelous sense of release that came over me, a wild singing sense of—of dissolution, all bonds gone, as if freedom were really possible. As if I could sprout wings and fly forever." He smiled again, that same wonderful smile. "So that insane poetry is in you as well, Dair! Who would have thought it." The smile faded. "But I cannot fly."

I cannot run with the pack, either, said Dair.

There was the real wound probed. Wolfwit ran strong in him, stronger than we could well imagine, but the great weaver was demanding his first loyalty; he was fated to be merely and dearly himself.

I want never to leave you again, he said to Frain, and I was hard put to keep my voice steady as I relayed the message. For it was not to be so, and perhaps he knew that even then. But it was the hope of his heart.

By the next day Dair was up and about a bit, scorning pain. We rubbed oil on his scabs to keep the skin from tightening. All the wounds were healing cleanly. The wolves sang at dusk again that night, and we watched Dair uneasily, but he ignored them.

Within several days we were walking along again, and Dair was nearly as supple as ever. That was to his own credit, for he made his limbs stretch and move in spite of pain, and after a while the pain left him. Scars remained. He reminded me more than ever of Trevyn, with his scars.

We went on through evergreen, oak and scrub pine and into tamarisk, and Frain seemed much the same troublesome youth as ever, and Dair none the worse for his escapade. But looking at him I sometimes felt a shadowy presentiment of further pain to come. Suffering for the son of a king.

Chapter Three

"I still do not understand about changing shapes," said Frain some few weeks later as we sat after food in the evening.

So that was why he had been so silent. I had thought he was tired, though of course he had not said so; he never complained of physical woes, and he had walked doggedly even when he had been weak from sickness. . . . I knew I was tired. It had been a tiring day, a hot and dusty one full of the sizzling sound of locusts in the acacia trees. But his question made me set weariness aside.

"It is a matter of taking not a false form but another true form," I started importantly. "If you were to change to—do you ever dream of being something?"

"A bird," he said. "A flying thing."

"Yes. Well, you would be. . . ." I lost my voice and my nerve. Already I was sorry we had gotten into this.

"A crippled bird," he said.

"Yes." I plunged on. "Well, when Dair became a horse, that was not a falsehood or a deception. It was Dair, the horse form of Dair. It was male, as he is. It was young, as he is. I would make an old gray mare."

"But how did he do it?" Frain pursued.

It was very difficult to explain anything to him. He thought in such stark terms, and I in far softer ones. There is a way of seeing a faint star by looking just to the side of it—but he had a mind like a sword, always darting swiftly to the point. I sighed.

"To be a creature—let us say a horse—"

Oh, and in this plodding language of his, too. It was awful, it made everything sound like blacksmithing.

"Well, to be a horse you must feel true desire to be a horse, and you must be in sympathy with the horse—a sort of liking, but more than liking—and then you must be able to let go of your human form."

"But—you mean completely become the other thing, body, self, everything?" I think he had envisioned the process as something akin to climbing into a dead skin. I nodded.

"Your human form is your own. In the same way, any other form you take will be your own. When you change forms, your essence goes with you, just as when you die it flies and becomes spirit."

"But—" He floundered. "But it is monstrous!" he burst out. "Changing shapes, I mean. It is—it is unnatural!"

How bound within walls he was, walls of his own making. "It is completely natural," I said. "The goddess is a shape changer. Aene can come to us in any form."

"But the goddess—"

He stopped, thinking. When he spoke again it was coolly and very carefully.

"Shamarra is a goddess," he said, "and she has been changed to a night bird by Adalis. If she were to learn this shape changing, might she be able to revert to her human form? But I suppose you are going to tell me that it is a skill that can be neither learned nor taught."

"Maybe so, Frain," I told him. "Maybe so."

I was oddly fond of him. Not in any lustful way, either, and that was unusual for me. But he was virgin, I could sense it, and I had known from the first that he was not for me; he was not strong enough. So I had taken to mothering him, I who had given up the only child of my own. And I hated to discourage any of his dreams, however absurd.

"It may be," I added, "that at the Source many things are possible."

"Maeve," he said wearily, "I was seven years in search of one legendary land and never found it, not really, and now am I to be seven years in search of another one? How can you be so sure about this Source of yours? I am a fool for letting you lead me off like this."

It was the first time he had admitted his doubt to me. I was honored that he trusted me enough to speak so honestly.

"What can you do but follow me?" I asked.

"Nothing." He smiled ruefully. "I need you and Dair to help me help Shamarra. I can see that now."

"Tell me more about this Shamarra," I said.

So he rehearsed the tale for me again. He told it more easily every time, and more dispassionately, in a ritual way, as priests sometimes recount sacred history, as if it were a legendary account and not at all a story of living, suffering flesh, least of all his own. Shamarra had been beautiful, passionate, and she had been violated, sorely wronged by the same person who had wronged Frain, his brother whom he loved, and he seemed to assume that love of Tirell constrained Shamarra as it did him, trapped her in a river of tears perhaps, ensnared her in a net of opposed emotions as it did him, but I knew better. He was more victim than she, I suspected. Once a healer, with no longer any health to spare, tangled in a puppyish attachment, unable to see clearly or hear the word of the goddess, bound in an eternal life of callow youthfulness, crippled by anger he could not vent or resolve—he thought of himself as Shamarra's rescuer, but I felt sure he would be able to help no one until he had helped himself. And his calm words, dropped like so many lifeless stones—

Only when he spoke of Fabron, his father, did he reveal some emotion.

"He healed the beast—well, he healed Tirell, in effect, and then the power left him and he was unable to heal me. He told me I was his son—and by the time he told me I had to leave him. I think it broke his heart." Frain's face quivered a little and he turned away from the firelight. Dair whined in sympathy and I looked on, I am afraid, with the keenest interest. Here I saw guilt as well as anger.

"You had to leave?" I prodded.

"Shamarra had left."

"But why could you not stay with Fabron?"

I knew why well enough, but I wanted him to know. He winced away from the question.

"I had to follow Shamarra."

It worked both for him and against him, that steadfastness of his—stubbornness, if you will. "Frain," I said with some degree of exasperation, "Shamarra is the least of it."

"She may be to you," he retorted, "but not to me."

"Listen." I edged closer to him, closer to the fire, trying to make him hear me by virtue of sheer proximity; how had he gotten me so intent on teaching him? "Listen, Frain.

It is real and true, all you say of Shamarra, but she is like one petal on a flower, one face to a standing stone, there is more to what has happened than her."

"Such as?"

"Such as spleen! Can you not see you were furious at Tirell for what he did? And at Fabron for leading you such a dance?"

"Perhaps." He shrugged it off. He could not deny his anger, but he would not feel it, either. "For whatever reason," he went on dryly, "I went back to Acheron. Back to the lake where it had all begun."

"And you saw the face in the water," I said.

"Yes." He shuddered violently. "Let us not speak of that, Maeve, or I'll have no sleep tonight."

Confound him, it was the thing above all others that needed to be spoken of! But I could not do it for him. I smothered a sigh of vexation and went on.

"And Shamarra had been turned into a night bird."

"Yes."

"What, exactly," I asked, "is a night bird?"

"A little, drab bird, creature of Vieyra, the hag, the death goddess. Many of them live in the Lorc Tutosel, the mountains of the night bird to the south of Vale." The words triggered a memory; I saw the haze of it in his eyes. "Wait," he said. "Listen." He leaned back and recited a sort of song.

"The night bird sings
Of asphodel;
The day bird wakes
And flaps his wings
And cannot fly
And lifts the cry
O Tutosel, Ai Tutosel!

The night bird sings
Of Vieyra's spell,
Of Aftalun's
Sweet hydromel
And dark chimes of
The wild bluebell
In reaches of high Tutosel."

There was more, about mortal's knell and the sad and flightless song of the dawn bird. Such a melancholy ditty.

The fire had burned down to ashes, and there seemed to be no more that either of us could say. Dair lay not in his blanket but on it, dozing, his limbs stretched out to one side, the attitude lupine even though he was in his human form. I sat and thought of the night bird. A small, dust-colored bird with a sweet, rippling, seductive voice.

"She should be flying with the flocks of Ascalonia," Frain burst out. He meant Shamarra, of course. I looked at him in some surprise.

"Can she not fly?"

"Yes, I suppose. But the proper form of the immortal is the swan, like the swan that always graced her lake."

"It is late," I said quietly. I got my blanket and swaddled myelf in it somewhat, eased myself down to the ground. My poor, stout body, it was not meant for all this walking and sleeping on stones. It ached. It longed to be something else, something strong and naked and free. . . . The moon was on the wax, and the wild thing or the breath of the goddess was stirring in me. The night bird flew through my thoughts.

It took a long time for Frain to go to sleep. When he was still at last, I sat up cautiously to find Dair sitting up and looking back at me. His ears twitched, listening to the night noises; human ears, they moved on his human head, and his nostrils moved as well. He smiled at me. He smiled very seldom, and I was glad, for it was a disconcerting rictus.

Shall we go together? he asked.

"All right," I whispered, "but we must stay close to Frain. There might be danger on the prowl for him."

You do not have to tell me that, he growled.

True enough, and enough of motherly nonsense. Wings flapped within my mind, and in a moment I was myself in flight, a small bird darting effortlessly upward, all aches forgotten. I perched on the high branch of a wych elm tree to look down on our campsite. A fluffy gray owl noiselessly swooped up and settled beside me.

Have you ever flown before? I asked Dair.

No. It is delightful. Do you think we are going to be able to change back in time?

The night bird did not know and did not care. Her thoughts were dark, her nature treacherous and musical in the minor key, selfish and sad and lovely as decadence always is. The owl was a night creature also, his reputation

85

for wisdom perhaps deserved. Dair proved less of a fool than I that night. But of that more in a moment.

We tilted our wings and fell into flight. We flew for the joy of it, circling above Frain's sleeping form, wheeling and gliding, till dawn. There is nothing like coming out of human self to refresh one. No sleep can match it. Out of self. . . . Frain stirred below me, and I did not care what he would think when he awoke, poor fool. To fly, just to let instinct bear one up, so easy—

So easy to die in an instant!

A falcon had appeared above me, diving down out of the dawn sky. I flashed toward the cover of an evergreen oak, but he was nearly on me, his talons reaching for my stubby tailfeathers. How had he gotten so close without my seeing him? Desperate, I plummeted to the ground and took refuge in my human form. Instead of veering off in consternation as I had expected it to, the raptor settled lightly beside me and became Dair. And he gave me that unnerving grin of his again.

"Dair, you beggar!" I exploded at him. "What do you mean! You frightened me half to death!"

What of Frain, if he had seen you? Dair growled back. *I have hurt him enough.*

Frain sat up, startled and sleepy. He blinked as he focused on us and identified us as the source of the uproar. "What in the world?" he exclaimed. We were naked, after all.

"Nothing." I swallowed my wrath, feeling suddenly sheepish as modesty and compunction returned to me. I reached hastily for my clothes, conscious of my thick body. "It is nothing at all, really," I told Frain vaguely. "We were out flying. . . ."

"On your besom? What do you use to rub yourself with?" He got up, laughing hollowly to himself.

"Now, stop that," I said, annoyed. "We were being birds, that is all."

"Indeed." He was still laughing softly, as if life were momentarily too funny for him to bear. He, earthbound with his crippled arm, he who dreamed of flight—cringing at the thought, I grew glad that he was laughing. I wondered how much anger the laughter hid.

"Do you want anything to eat?" I asked him, solicitous.

"Who could eat?" he chortled. "Let us be getting on."

We broke camp and trudged off eastward. It was midmorning before Frain seemed entirely his sober self again and we stopped for a bite of bread.

"This Shamarra," I said to him. "You say she is an aspect of the death goddess."

"Yes. In a very real way I seek death." He said it baldly, with no great drama.

"She must be rather heartless," I ventured.

"Yes." Oh, the things he was not telling me!

"The form of the night bird," I said, "it suits her."

"Yes. I know it."

He was maddening. "Would it be too dense of me," I inquired with some asperity, "to ask why you are not content to just let her be?"

He seemed startled by the question. "Well, she turned friendlier toward the last," he said hesitantly.

I was losing my temper. *"Frain,"* I warned.

"I love her," he declared.

"Frain, I could scream!" I shouted at him. "The real reason, if you please!"

He kept silence for some time. I thought at first that he was sulking, but looking at him I could see that he was thinking, struggling with truth. My ill humor vanished. I waited.

"This condition of mine," he said softly at last.

"Yes?"

"I doomed it on myself when I set foot in her lake. The passions I felt then will not fade. They are all still mine, still and forevermore. That is why I have not been able to grow—or change—"

I gaped at him. He met my gaze quite levelly, the lines of his face tight and grim.

"But—she *let* you?" I gasped.

"She let me. She wanted a faithful pet, I think." His words were calm and bleak. "I am in thrall," he said.

Chapter Four

We passed out of Tokar and through some other countries and into nameless lands, until not only the boundaries of kingdoms but even the nature of the earth changed. We came to the end of forest and onto something different, some sort of upland plateau. From a high, blunt promontory at the edge of it we looked out across a muddle of rocky hills, mostly sheep pasturage, with stone-walled garths on the summits. To me the outlook was bleak. We had not run afoul of brigands, not yet; Dair had seen to that. But we were out of food, and there would be no more wild grapes to eat, and no more deer for Dair's hunting.

I fingered my modest gold necklace and sighed. By night I could be a prowling wildcat under a full moon, or the wisent with wicked curving horn, or the she-wolf, or even the witch Frain had laughingly accused me of being. But by day I was very much the woman, and I hated to barter away the jewelry my parents had left me. Still, when one is on one's way to the Source there seems little sense in holding anything back.

"Let us go there," I said, pointing out the most prosperous-looking garth. We strode off single file down the slope.

We spent the night by a warm hearth. They were hospitable, those lonesome garth folk, even toward so oddly assorted a trio of strangers. In the morning we left with a goodly supply of bread, cheese, apples and dried mutton. And without my necklace, of course.

And so it went until nearly midwinter. It did not snow, we were too far south for that, but we were often glad of the shelter of a stone homestead those chill nights, and I traded away my bracelet and ring. Oh, we met with the occasional rebuff, with hostility from time to time, even with danger—there were rough folk on those moorlands, too, it turned out. But what mostly happened was steady, silent days of walking and evenings of quiet talk, the bond between Dair and Frain and my motherly affection for the pair of them, and aches and blisters, and grumbling on rainy days, and a feeling that each of us could depend on the others. Even Frain, our cripple—Dair and I were protective of him, and he accepted it; he had never had proper mothering, I think. But there was far more to him than there seemed to be.

I remember particularly one time when Dair was off hunting for rabbits amongst the gorse bushes somewhere. It was dusk, the day between dog and wolf, as the country-folk would say, a threatening time of day, and two strangers with swords suddenly appeared at our campfire. They looked at us and laughed.

"A cripple and a woman!" one said. "And not much good to be had from either of them, it seems."

"We'll take it out on the female," said the other, leering. "Though at her age I doubt if she is still tight enough to afford much pleasure."

Frain got up wearily. Neither of us was very much afraid. We knew that I would undergo a change when I became angry enough, probably into wolf form, and then those men would learn the meaning of bloodshed. But I suppose Frain's pride was stung—he had pride, though he usually kept it private—so he stood up to confront the pair of brigands, and they laughed anew, waiting with delight to see what he would do.

"Scum," he remarked offhandedly, and then he moved with eagle speed. He jerked his body so that his left arm, the useless one, swung out and hit the nearer robber across the face with a fishy slap. Startled and angered, the man put up his sword, and I squeaked; it cut into Frain's arm. But on the instant Frain had ahold of the sword hilt with his good hand. He wrenched it away from his enemy. One quick backhand blow to an unprotected throat and the man was dead. Just as quickly Frain turned and parried the blow the other brigand was aiming at his neck.

This fellow was ready for a fight. He had his shield up, and Frain had none, and blood dripped down from his dangling, wounded arm. I began to think of shouting for

Dair—he was already in his wolf form, of course. But I did not. I merely sat with my mouth open. Frain handled his sword with astounding force and skill. He was breathtaking, nothing short of magnificent—I could have watched him all night. Blade clanged against blade ever faster, but Frain remained untouched. All the while he pricked his enemy with his swordtip, nudged and caressed him with it in a grim game of power. He could have killed him any of half a dozen times, and the man knew it. Pallid and sweating, the brigand stumbled back, turned and fled. Frain stood and let him go.

I came out of my stupor, scrambled up and hurried over to him. "Mighty Mothers, Frain!" I exclaimed. At the same time Dair came running up, four-legged.

I saw a very scared sort of robber run by, he said. *What has happened—Name of the Lady, Frain!*

"Name of the Lady, Frain!" I translated, tugging at him. I got him to sit down, and I ripped bandaging for the slash on his arm. Dair sat on his tail, whimpering.

"Save your sympathy, both of you," Frain grumped. "There is no feeling in that arm, no pain, as I knew full well before I presented it to be sliced."

"Then why are you trembling?" I retorted. He was very pale and shaking violently. I wrapped the wound tightly to stop the bleeding.

Why didn't you call me! Dair appealed. Both of us ignored him.

"Why didn't you *tell* me you were such a swordsman!" I snapped at Frain in mock anger, trying to make him smile.

"No. Please." He turned away his face, trembling harder than ever, and curled himself into a taut ball. I put a blanket around him, puzzled and worried.

It is not pain, Dair told me. *He is terrified.*

"But why?"

Because—he has used the sword, the weapon of wrath. Dair went over and sat by Frain, pressed against him. In a moment Frain gave a dry sob and took the wolf into his one-armed embrace, hiding his face in the thick fur of Dair's neck.

"We have to get away from here," I said uneasily. "That robber who lived might come back with more."

Frain got up and went about the work of breaking camp, his face tight, twitching. We set off at once, in the dark and without sleep—I am sure Frain would not have been able to sleep in any event. We left the dead outlaw slowly stiffening on the ground behind us, his sword at his side. Dair led us through the night in wolf form, very warily, while Frain and I walked quite silently at his heels. But no harm befell us that night.

Just before dawn Frain spoke at last.

"I had thought the sword skill had left me," he said very softly. His tone was not one of rejoicing.

"You thought you had gotten rid of it, you mean?" I teased gently. I could not see his face, but I doubt if he smiled.

"No. A few years ago, some time after I left Vale, I got in a—well, a contest, and I was beaten so badly I had to be nursed for a month. I really wanted to be killed, but by bad fortune the man was merciful." His tone was hard.

"You were splendid," I said. "What troubles you so?"

"Bad dreams—and faces in the night. All the trees have eyes tonight." He shivered.

"Let us sit and watch the dawn," I said.

We rested. I could tell that the light comforted Frain. I glanced at him from time to time, thinking.

"Have you heard the tale of Eterlane, the hero?" I asked him, finally.

"The hero's name is Aftalun."

"Aftalun, Feridun, Eterlane, it is all the same," I said impatiently. "The hero is the one who confronts the dragon."

"My brother Tirell talked with dragons," Frain said.

I did not want to hear any more about Tirell. I gave him a sharp look.

"With Aftalun it was a swimming dragon," he added with some small interest. "He had to dive. . . ."

"Deep in the water, the flood, until his fire was victorious or quenched," I finished for him. Aftalun was the sun—I felt sure of it from the way Frain watched the rays break over the horizon.

"What of Eterlane?" he asked after a while.

"For Eterlane the dragon was in a dungeon."

I took my time and told the tale. There was once a terribly poor kingdom, I said, hagridden by famine and plague and all kinds of misfortune, and this was all blamed on the dragon. It had been with the kingdom for ages, and no one could slay it; the dragon was invincible. The only thing that could be done with it was to keep it out of sight, hidden deep in its hole, shut into its dark lair. So there it lurked, with the whole weight of the castle over it. But it was prophesied that one day a prince would come of age who would be able to deal with it.

The prince had lived with the roar of the unseen dragon from his earliest days. And when the time came for his rite of passage, in which he would receive his true-name, a hag appeared at the castle gates, keening. The king himself went out to see her.

"What are you grieving for?" he asked her. He suspected her of being more than she appeared to be, and he was right. She stopped in midwail and glared at him.

"For human folly," she snapped. "Where is that boy?"

The king called his son. "What do you wish with him?" he asked when the prince stood before them.

"I am to marry him," the old crone said, "when I have taught him how to face the dragon."

King and prince stood aghast at the idea and refused the bargain, and the old woman went away wailing as before. But no true-name came to the prince, and no true love either, and no good to the stricken kingdom, for the year after. And then the hag came again, and was refused again, and so it went for the next year, and the next, until at last the prince saw that the dragon had to be faced, though his father still trembled at the idea.

"I accept your offer," he said when the hag came again.

"Empty the castle," she told him.

It was done, and he turned to descend to the lair.

"What weapon should I take with me?" he asked the goddess, for it was she.

"Nothing except thoughts. I will give you three. The white dove casts a dark shadow. In the heart of the rose is a worm. Night fades into day and day into night; embrace them."

"Is that all?"

"And your true-name. It is Eterlane."

It was a good name. The sound of it gave him warmth and courage as he walked away.

The passage to the dragon's lair was strait and dark. The prince had to feel his way along, groping ever downward. At last there was a dim reddish light, and Eterlane stopped short. The glow came from a toothy mouth and two nostrils like embers. The bulk behind them loomed large, formless and terrifying.

"What do you want with me?" the dragon asked.

There was nothing Eterlane could do except answer it.

"I want you to stop this drought and plague and famine," he said shakily.

"Misfortune?" inquired the dragon slowly. "But which of us is to blame? Let me look at you in the light."

"What?" Eterlane exclaimed.

"Let me out to the light, I say." The dragon started forward.

Eterlane was badly scared. He had left all the portals open behind him for his own escape, and now the dragon would get loose—what a fool he had been to let that hag send him down here without a weapon, he thought. He snatched up a stone from the floor and hurled it. The dragon grunted and sent him staggering back with a blow of its great clawed foot. Eterlane shouted and stamped at the claws, and another push sent him stumbling back again.

So they went, with the dragon shoving and slithering and the hero fighting punily all the way, until they came out of the dungeon into the granaries and guardrooms. Eterlane could have gotten himself a weapon there, but he had begun hazily to realize that he had not been harmed. He ran up the steps to the sunlit throne room, panting and wondering. The dragon followed, and at the dais Eterlane turned to face it.

The dragon came out into the full light with a crunch of scales. It was terribly ugly, gray and ulcerous and sickening, like a bloated snake. It stared at Eterlane with bleary yellow eyes.

"Why have you hurt me?" it asked him.

"What are you?" cried Eterlane, terribly confused. "And what do you have to do with me?"

"My name is Eterlane," said the dragon, "and I have been confined in the dark because you hate me. Why do you hate me?"

Eterlane stood for a moment stunned. Then, "How can I hate one who bears my true-name?" he whispered. He walked up to the gray slimy beast and greeted it as a second self.

"So you see," I said, "all that was necessary was for him to accept."

The dragon was anger, of course, or any one of the hidden things that poison people's lives. I could tell that the tale made Frain uncomfortable. He did not understand it and did not want to.

"And the hag?" he inquired after looking at the sunrise for a while.

"Eterlane kept his promise and wed her, and she turned fair and blooming. She was his kingdom, you see, or the womanform of it, and when he took the throne fortune flowered once again for his people. But no good could come to him or to them until he had faced the thing he feared."

Frain got up with a gesture of negation or disgust. "Let us go on," he said.

He slept only fitfully for some time thereafter, and I noticed that Dair seemed constantly on the alert, for what sort of trouble I was not sure. But there was no more need of swordsmanship.

Chapter Five

The hills gradually lowered and lowered, falling away in front of us. We walked over them through the shortening days and the solstice and the lengthening days, eastward, always eastward, following the path of the swimming sun. We began to grow aware of a sort of shine far in front of us, and as we drew nearer to it we thought it was a great inland sea. But how could that be, with water becoming harder and harder to find? The garths were fewer and farther apart, their wells more grudging, the land arid. Only dry and twisted prickly things grew on it. No longer could we find the crabapples and wild pears that had sustained us somewhat.

We are going to have to live on lizards, said Dair. *That is a desert ahead.*

So it was, a sea of gleaming sand with waves and ripples that slowly moved under the touch of the wind. Rocks stood irregularly scattered, carved into anvil shapes by the blowing sand. The warmthless winter sun pounded down, so harsh that the light hurt our eyes. Nothing seemed to live or move on that expanse except wind, sun shadow, and sand.

And we did not have much food or water. And the call of my unseen Source led us straight across the waste.

We camped on the last dry, rocky hill to consider.

"You two could turn into eagles or something and fly right over it," Frain said. "In fact, I have been wondering for some time why you struggle along as humans at all. You could just fly away."

It's not so simple, grumbled Dair.

"What?"

"It's not so simple," I translated. "Anyway," I added, "we would not want to leave you."

"That's nice," he said, a trifle sarcastically. "But one of you could turn bird and go scouting. Or you could be horses and let me ride you across. Why is it not so simple?"

I tried to explain. It was always awkward talking to him because he understood only the crude human languages. "Magic cannot be used, really," I said, "It comes as Trevyn's dreams come, or rain—when it will. Usually only for sheerest fun or in time of greatest need."

"Don't we need to get across there?" Frain asked. "Or at least, you say we do."

"We do." I ignored his surliness. "But we are not dying, are we?"

"Not yet."

"Listen," I said. "When you had the power, the healing power, would you use it to cure a hangnail?"

"No, of course not," he retorted stiffly. "I used it only if someone was very ill or gravely hurt. And then it would shoot through me like lightning and leave me weak for days afterward. . . ." Frain suddenly looked sheepish. "I was not thinking," he said. "Do you two bear something like that, some sort of—well, penalty?"

"No," I had to admit. "No, nothing like that. But the point is, you knew the power was not to be used for—oh, warts and things."

"And you say this is a wart we are sitting on now." Frain grinned at Dair, and Dair barked out his gruff laugh. The two of them got along even better than usual when they were baiting me.

"All right," I snapped. "So what do we do? I am not about to force either of you to come onto that desert with me."

"That is where you are going?" asked Frain.

"For myself, I have no choice."

"I cannot begin to comprehend this Source of yours." He looked at me, sighed and shook his head, then shrugged. "Well, I am not about to force Dair to choose between us," he said. "I will come with you."

Thank you, said Dair, a low and heartfelt murmur. For once Frain seemed to understand. He smiled at his friend.

We ventured out onto the sand the next day, naive and undersupplied. At least it was wintertime, so we did not suffer from burning heat. But the footing was soft and the walking difficult. And we rationed ourselves severely; we

96

suffered from hunger and thirst. We walked as steadily as we could, often walking half the night, to cross as much desert as we could before we ran out of water. Dair left the food and most of the water to Frain and me. He ate lizards and things, as he had said he would. I could not do that. Nor could I change to wolf form as readily as he did. I was more stodgily human than he. I kept scanning the glare of the horizon, hoping we would find nomads or gypsies who had learned how to live on this wasteland, or a sign of ending to it, or water somehow; anything.

Within the week the day came, inexorably, when we were entirely out of water. At once our remaining food became a matter of indifference. Already our lips were cracked and our eyes burning from privation. No one had energy even to quarrel—a bad state of affairs. We stumbled along. The sand seemed to cling to our feet and drag us down, and I for one wanted to yield to it, merely to lie in it and rest, perhaps forever.

"Time for a change," Frain mumbled through thickened lips.

I shook my head, not in negation but in despair. I could not begin to summon a dream or a formthought for change—I had not realized how much vitality was needed to make the change. I felt entrapped in my human self, mired and helpless.

"Trust the goddess," I told Frain, telling myself, really.

We walked through most of that night and stumbled through the next day, hoping to find an end to the endless sand, but of course there was none. When nightfall came again we all by unspoken consent lay down where we were and went to sleep without making camp of any kind. Blessed sleep, it was our only flight. We slept deeply. And sometime in the formless darkness we were all startled awake by a tremendous crack of thunder, and a torrent of rain fell down on us.

Rain! Dair sprang up and burst into a sort of barbaric dance that was rendered all the more savage by dark drum of thunder and flicker of lightning. Frain, quiet soul that he was, merely lay on his back, stretched himself luxuriously and opened his mouth wide to catch any drops that might happen to fall into it. I found our packs and spread out all our cooking things to catch the water.

"Stop that," I shouted at Dair, who was still dancing. "Sit down. If you knock anything over I'll pound you."

He sat, and after a moment's thought I got out our

blankets and spread them open as well, and the clothes that Dair never wore, and I opened the packs themselves into crude cups—anything to catch the rain. The thunder subsided and the downpour became a steady, glorious shower. I let it soak my hair, put the dripping ends into my mouth and sucked them. Such a marvel, rain! Well, it was the season for it, after all. When the occasional desert rain came, it would be at this time of year. But I could not help feeling it was a special favor of the goddess meant for us. And given in a way worthy of her, too—no sunny offerings, hers, but always the thunder startle, the night-time scare. I smiled. The darkness was turning to dawn, and the rain had turned to trickle and drop. By the first pale gold rays of light we could see the rainclouds scudding away westward.

We set to work pouring caught rainwater into our flasks. There was not really very much, just enough for a few days or perhaps another thirsty week, but we were most grateful for it. We wrung the water out of our blankets into our cooking pans. It was rather dirty, but we drank it. Then we sucked the wet cloth. Then we packed up our things and walked away eastward, nearly merry. Once again we had no thought for food. Water was enough.

Those were lovely days. All sorts of fragile and astounding blossoms burst out of the sand so fast that we could almost see them growing. They spread delicate petals, dropped their seeds and died in the time it took the sand to dry. Creatures came out too, from dens beneath rocks or far underground, toads and turtles and little rodents, to transact a lifetime's business in the space of those few days. We feasted on turtle eggs. Dair ate stranger things than that. But within the week all was gone, and so was our water, or nearly so. And our clothes were dry and the sand was as dry and lifeless as before.

There were mountains on the horizon to the north and east. We watched them warily, scarcely daring to mention them to each other at first, thinking they might be some sort of illusion, they shimmered so. But they grew closer as we walked. And by the time we were due for our second bout with despair, lips parched, tongues thickened and flasks empty, it became apparent that we were going to pass them by to the southward. One evening near sunset, when the slanting light defined every contour of them, Frain abruptly sat down and studied them intently. Per-force, Dair and I stood still and studied them as well.

"It has to be," Frain said softly. "I am very weary but not yet insane, and I say there could not be any other such mountains in the world. The feathery shapes of them, the golden stone and the silver aspens on the lower slopes— those are the Lorc Tutosel, the mountains of the night bird. On the other side of them lies Vale." His voice was vibrant with yearning.

Let us go see, said Dair excitedly.

"No!" I said, too sharply. "Our way lies eastward."

"There is water at those mountains," Frain stated dreamily. "Deep pools lie in the hollows of their roots. But that is the least of the tug. . . ." He got up. "Maeve, I begin to understand the strong call of your Source," he said. "I see my homeland, and I must go to it. Will you come with me?"

"I must go east," I mumbled.

"Come as far as the foothills, find water and then go east. Dair?" He turned to my son. Dair nodded emphatically.

Mother, come, Dair urged me. *Your death lies eastward unless you do.*

They were seductive, the pair of them. They beckoned and coaxed and pulled at me. And of course it was only common sense to make the detour. Though common sense had had little to do with this quest from the beginning.

"All right," I sighed. I shouldered my pack and we trudged off northward. How odd it felt to be going northward. I bent sideways, as Frain bent toward his withered arm to balance the good. But I bent because I was crossing a strong, unseen and soundless tide.

We reached the mountains a few days later. We were wobbling, nearly crawling, from thirst and exhaustion. But everything was just as Frain had said it would be: deep in the fold of the first sheer slope we found our water. A small riot of tousled greenery surrounded the little rill. It seeped down a beard of moss into a small brown pool, then meandered away and disappeared within a dozen feet. To us it was a heavenly fountain, a vision of delight. We all drank deeply, then lay down where we were and slept.

In the morning we awoke to clamorous birdsong. Birds wintered in these southern woods, it seemed. The aspens all around were alive with birds, every kind and color of bird, including grouse. I had thought Frain was still asleep, but I saw his hand move stealthily to grasp a stone. In one swift motion he sat up and threw it with startling speed and force. A grouse fell, stunned and flapping, and he ran to secure it. Dair watched, wide-eyed.

99

But—when has he grown able to gather game?

"See how much good it does me to be home?" Frain brought us our breakfast, grinning.

We ate the grouse and the mushrooms that grew around the pool and a few snails as well; we were ravenous. We foraged all day rather than traveling. In the next mountain hollow we found a larger pool with fish. We caught them in Dair's unused shirt. They were tiny things, and we ate them bones and all, we were so starved. Dair changed to wolf form at the sight of them and ate them raw rather than waiting for us to cook them. At dusk I saw him digging for frogs with his paws. Later yet he went off to see if he could find us anything warmblooded.

"We must turn eastward tomorrow," I said reluctantly. I felt not nearly satisfied, my belly still rumbling, and these mountains seemed like paradise after the desert. Frain merely nodded.

In the night the goddess sent rain—now that we no longer needed it, as might be expected of her. Nor was it any gentle rain. Thunder so loud that I thought the mountains above us were splitting, the very rocks roaring, and rain sheeting down heavy as ice, and green and orange lightning—I properly cowered, a new experience for me.

"Winter thunder, the world's wonder," Frain chanted, trying to ease the tension; the night felt as though the very air were stretched taut, thin skin on the drumhead of thunder. Then there sounded an eerie screech through the pitch darkness and pouring rain, and wild laughter veered through the sky. In the sudden silence that followed shriek and thunder I heard Frain's sharp intake of breath.

"The Luoni are out," he said.

"The Luoni?" I inquired weakly, still cowering.

"The—they are great, ugly birds with the heads of starved women. They live on the crags. They will not harm the living, they only look at you with eyes like—like fate, but they harry the dead. And they smell their game tonight."

We sat up all night in unspoken fear. The next morning the sun came up sullenly, a clot of dried blood. Frain looked up at the mountaintops, tired, half fearful but keen-eyed.

"I just have to go up," he said.

"I must go east," I protested. "I sense the wrath of the goddess already. Make your decision, Frain, whether you are going with me."

"How can I decide until I know where I stand? Look."

He pointed toward a notch in the towering peaks. "There is a pass. From it I will be able to look beyond, to see if it is truly Vale there, and you will be able to scan your way eastward. It will only take a few days to get there, and then I will make my decision. All right?"

"All right," I muttered, though I knew he was leading me a dance. I could bear to part from him, if need be, but I could not bear to part from him churlishly.

We climbed up through the aspens and the rock that lay among the aspens. Frain was in a state of suppressed excitement, color riding high in his cheekbones, his brown eyes sparkling. The thought of a look at his home after all the years had blotted out all other considerations for him, all fear and caution. He climbed tirelessly, sometimes surging far ahead of Dair and me. If he had had two good arms I think he could have left us behind altogether. As it was, he set a hard pace, and by evening we had reached the heather above the treeline. We could look back over the desert we had traversed. In fact, we sat and looked in fascination tinged with terror. For the sun was going down flanked by ominous dogs.

I have never seen that before, said Dair.

"Nor have I," I mumbled.

"I have heard of it," Frain said in hushed tones. "The sun is called Aftalun in my country; he is a great golden immortal, first Sacred King and first to die, he who wed Adalis. He gave man fire and metal and cattle and staghounds. Dogs."

The sky was naked of clouds, glazed and glaring with orange sunlight. The sun dogs were squat, off-colored ruddy flares to either side of the main orb.

A rumble sounded in the darkening sky.

"Let us see if we can get some sleep," sighed Frain.

But we did not sleep, not with the whistlings and cracklings and weird shoutings in the sky. A ball of fire leaped over the mountaintops like a giant hound, and there was blood on the hazy moon. I huddled under my blanket, watching, and even Dair stayed close to our small fire. A blazing streak of light—had that been a comet?

"Comets fly when great men die," said Frain softly, fear in his voice. He was thinking, I believe, of Tirell.

Before dawn had well broken he urged us to start again up the mountainside.

"You are leading us into peril," I argued. "Can you not sense it?"

"I sense omens, portents. I must find out what is happening."

"I sense the anger of the goddess," I retorted. "It fills the air like lightning."

"One more day," he said. "Please." And I could not refuse him.

Chapter Six

It was dusk, the day between dog and wolf, when we topped the pass.

"There," Frain breathed, panting from the climb.

I jumped and shuddered, not even looking at the distant landscape of what might have been Vale, for I was having my first confrontation with a Luona. A great, dirt-colored, dumpy-looking bird clung to the rock with yellowish claws, and drab hair streamed down around its wings from its human head—the head of an emaciated woman. It looked straight at me with its sunken eyes, facing me at shoulder height, not much more than an arm's length away.

"*Laifrita thae*," I greeted it hoarsely. Any living thing deserves a greeting. It did not answer; it only stared at me, an appraising look that was very hard to bear. At my side, Dair also felt that stare and moved uneasily. But Frain ignored the ugly thing, gazing out over the fallow folds of land.

"It *is* Vale," he said in a hushed voice. "I can see the towers of Ky-Nule—just on the horizon, there." He pointed the place out to us. "I know them well," he assured us, as if our silence doubted him. "That is my father's court city—Fabron, I mean. And look, there is a hunt."

Far below us at the foothills we could see pennons and movement. The huntsmen were so distant we could not hear horns or hounds. The hunt was all spread and straggling, as if something had led it a long chase. Frain watched the faraway horsemen with fascination, but I turned my eyes to the sky. It was darkening, the sun had already set, and we could not camp here on this open, windy pass with those dreadful Luoni in attendance—

others had flapped down to join the first. They stared at me in their turn, and I felt as if all the eyes of heaven were on me as well. We would have to find shelter somewhere. There seemed to be two promising close-set rocks a little way below—

"Fabron!" Frain gasped. "It is Fabron!"

I looked. A rider had appeared halfway up the mountain, much closer than the others, flashing out from behind jutting rocks and gorse and driving his horse at a breakneck pace. It was easy to see how Frain had known him even at the distance. He was burly, full-bearded, golden-helmed, a splendid figure of a man, his dark velvet clothing studded with many clasps and brooches and ornamental chains. He gave off a rich metallic sparkle as he rode, and so did his steed, the harness well trapped—in a moment his quarry came into view before him. It was a deer, and such a magnificent deer—a stag, I thought, though I found out later that the roe deer of Vale also bear antlers—a great, shining, high crowned ruler of deer, silvergold—the color alone would have been enough to make men kill. Up and up the mountain it came, with Fabron urging his horse along behind, the poor steed slick with sweat, every inch of it. All the other horsemen and even the hounds had long since given up.

On they came, straight toward us, the royal in pursuit of the regal. Frain stood oddly silent. I glanced over at him and saw some sort of struggle making confusion of his face.

"I—let us go," he muttered. "If he sees me—"

"You don't want to greet your father?" I asked, astonished.

"No. I don't. I—" Then he went pale, aghast. "Do you hear it?" he stammered.

I heard it, a faint, sourceless, incorporeal ringing, thousands of thin and tiny bells sounding in a minor mode.

"The chimes of the bluebell are said to be an omen of death," Frain whispered. "And what else could that be?"

There were no bluebells about, not in winter. So much the worse. I felt sick. There had been far too many omens of late.

"Whose death?" I snapped.

Frain did not answer, his eyes wide and fixed on Fabron. Hunter king and hunted creature had almost reached the twin stones that stood stark just below us, their bases in a pool of deepening shadow by now. Frain seemed to notice them for the first time.

"Kedal and Kedur," he moaned. "The betrayed ancestral staghounds of Vaire. Oh, no. Fabron. . . ."

It was not a shout of warning; it was no more than a murmur. The deer appeared between the twin rocks, passed through them in one floating leap. Fabron appeared on his lathered, laboring horse. Eerily I noticed the staghound crest on his helm. He forced his reluctant steed into the narrow gap—

And the deer whirled and turned on him, but in that instant it was no longer the deer. It still wore antlers, its crown, but it was all flash of teeth; it was wolf, staghound, hell hound, catamount and bear, a fluid, shifting, monstrous and bestial snarling thing that barred the way, a horned horror, all ferocity. It was feathered dragon, antlered serpent, writhing—there was a scream, or screaming. It could have been the apparition or the terrified horse or the triumphant Luoni, or Frain, or even me. I cannot tell. The dusk was full of screaming. Then Fabron fell.

His death was very quick. And it was not the fearsome beast that killed him, either. His own horse did all the evil work, poor creature. Unable to flee in the narrow slot between monoliths, it reared and toppled backward and smashed its rider against the stone. Fabron fell to the ground, and the horse heaved itself up and ran off down the mountainside. The Luoni flew off, too, swooping and shrieking, pursuing the departing soul.

And the staghorned monster was gone as if it had never been. A small, sooty bird flew up from the ground where it had stood and perched on the left-hand stone.

Frain had stood frozen while his father met his doom. But a moment later he moved and ran scrambling down the steep rock toward the shadow where Fabron lay. I started after him too late to stop him. I strongly sensed danger—the very air inaudibly rang of danger. But Dair was off, too, right after Frain, down the jagged slope at the risk of his bare human skin, and I followed the pair of them more slowly.

I found Frain examining Fabron. "His neck is broken," he was saying numbly as I drew near. "And he was trampled, but—I think that came after."

He's dead, Dair told me.

"I know that," I snapped. I found it hard to be sympathetic when something was causing the short gray hairs on the back of my neck to rise. From just behind me there came a rippling, gelid laugh. I turned, Dair rose, Frain rose, we all stood as if we were puppets. Only Fabron, dead, dead on the ground, remained indifferent.

The most beautiful of women stood there, a woman like a silver flow of water, where the fatal beast had stood.

"Shamarra!" Frain breathed.

I heard and struggled to comprehend—was this his goddess? She was supposed to be his beloved; how could she have done this to him? But then I looked at her and understood, felt a shock of recognition, a certain disturbing empathy, even. She was the feral one. She was the wild thing, an elemental, the essence of all wildness in search of vengeance on the ways of men. How was I to say that Frain must not love her? She was a creature comrade, a fellow. More, she was myself, or in me, part of me, to my dismay. I had felt that feminine anger. . . . And she was magnificent, exquisite and awesome. I could have gone to my knees and worshiped her. And her singleness of passion gave her immense magic. I knew at once that I was no match for her. As for Frain, he was a pawn at her command.

She spoke. I learned later what was said, for the language of Vale was strange to me. At the time I heard only her cold, numbing tone, wash of words as cold as a mountain stream.

"Well, Frain, of all people!" She laughed again, the tinkling, liquid laugh of icy water. "How quaint of you to come."

"You—" Frain could not speak; his voice was wooden, splintering. Shamarra nodded almost coyly.

"I have found my human form again, yes, and many others, and powers you cannot dream of. I have grown. You have had fantasies of rescuing me from my cruel fate, have you not?" She smiled benignly. "How very sweet of you."

"You—why have you killed Fabron?"

"Oh, your father." She cast a cool glance on the corpse. "Poor fool. It was because he would not help me kill Tirell."

Frain made a sound that was not speech, a strangled, stunned and questioning sound. Shamarra went on readily. She seemed quite willing to talk to him; she condescended to him, as it were. In a sense she treated him as an old

106

friend. She ignored Dair and me. I have never felt so glad to be ignored.

"Vengeance," she said quite quietly. "You know what he did to me, Frain—I must have vengeance. It patterns all my days and dreams, my waking and my sleeping. I have worked toward vengeance these eight long years. Luring you away was only an easy first step, my pet. Then I had a setback, and I had to find my way out of that night bird form—weary work, but my powers have only increased by it. Lately I have taken council with Raz. He is only too glad to challenge Tirell now that I have showed him what I can do for him, how I can turn the river in its course and make it run against Melior. And there is that fool Sethym. He is always eager for fresh-spilled blood."

Raz and Sethym were canton kings of Vale, as Fabron had been.

"And I felt sure I could persuade Fabron to join cause with us," Shamarra went on. "He has been very bitter against Tirell on your account, young my lord, as I intended him to be. At first he seemed willing enough to turn traitor, but lately some absurd notion of loyalty has taken hold of him. And of course I could not have that. So—" She shrugged her delicate shoulders, indicating the body which lay behind us with a slight movement of one pearly bare foot.

Frain stepped forward, and Dair and I reached out with one accord to stop him. Shamarra was very dangerous— any fool could see that. He must not get too close to her. I could feel him trembling, perhaps not with fear.

"But you must not kill Tirell!" he cried at her. "You can't! He is—he is True King!"

"I can't!" she mimicked, mocking him. "Mustn't kill Tirell! And what of his death that dwells in your heart, that makes your teeth grow long with yearning for his blood? I know how you dream of dispatching him when you dare to let yourself dream."

Frain stood as white as if he had been stabbed.

"It is all right, you can tell me! I am the dark lake of death; have you forgotten?" She spread her slender hands. In that moment she seemed more his friend than in any other.

"You are hateful!" Frain blurted. "Ghoul—" Convulsively he started toward her, his one fist clenched. We

107

restrained him. I felt very frightened at the slight stirring of her face, shadow on deep water—very frightened.

"So I am a ghoul, now," she said softly, too softly. "I suppose I am. But, Frain, I will not kill Tirell quite yet."

Life's breath seemed to have left us all. We waited for the final blow.

"I intend to dishonor him first." Cruel delight was in Shamarra's every word, a catlike, nearly playful delight. "Raz has a scheme to make his wife leave him. And there are ways to make his warriors turn against him, and his officers, and even the people of his hall. I want him to see quite clearly his doom as it draws near." She smiled again, the most warmthless of smiles. "And I want it to break his heart. I may even be able to make some use of you, my pup." The epithet came out hurtfully; her eyes glittered with grisly inspiration. "I may let you slay him for me yourself!"

It was nearly full dark. Shamarra shone in the gloom like so much pale ice. Her hair was a shimmering waterfall, her dress a silver flow, her features smooth as lily-leaves without being at all soft, and for all her beauty and for all my soul's sympathy with her, I felt weak with terror of her. The purity of her wrath had filled her with insuperable power.

"Alys!" I screamed out. "Alys, come here at once, I need you. Come, hurry!"

Shamarra took the two steps to Frain—she seemed to flow rather than walk. She raised one lotuslike hand and laid the fair fingers on his arm, taking possession of him as completely as if she had bound him in chains.

"You are mine," she said. "Follow me." He stood in helpless horror.

"To think I once longed for those words," he whispered. "But you enslaved me years ago."

Then Alys came down to the mountaintop, and all things stopped as they were.

Chapter Seven

Frain saw her as an enormous white swan with wings out-spread, and Dair saw her as a huge and blinding argent moon. But I saw her as the massive Great Mother, she who sits like a sphere of white marble, unmoved by the world's pleading.

At times of great trouble, peculiar vexations take hold of a person. Frain turned from the apparition and looked at me fixedly.

"That is the goddess," he stated rather than asked.

"Yes," I whispered.

"I know it is. I met her in Isle. You called her?"

"Yes," I whispered hurriedly. "I hope she might help you. For myself I have little hope. Shhh!"

"Great galloping damnation!" he shouted out loud. "You mean I've tramped over half the world looking for her, and she was in Vale all the time?"

"Of course she was!" I hissed at him fiercely. "Now hush, before she blasts you!"

Dair added his voice to the muted uproar. *Confound it,* he complained, *wasn't one goddess trouble enough? Now we have two to deal with.*

Shamarra stood frozen in the presence of Alys as we had stood before her. Alys was far more dangerous than she but, I hoped, less malicious.

"Silence, Dair." The voice came from everywhere, chill-ingly, but the tone was not unkind. She liked Dair, I knew at once. His father was Trevyn, her favorite, after all, and Dair was a marvel in himself. "Silence, Frain." She sounded merely bored. "Maeve." Suddenly there was thunder in the tone, and fire flickered over the mountaintop. "Come here."

I walked forward about a half dozen steps, then stopped. I could not force myself any nearer. I have never felt so craven.

"What," said Alys, "are you doing here." It was not so much a question as a rebuke and an accusation. I bowed my head.

"We came to find water—" I whispered like a girl child, I, a woman of more years than I cared to count.

"Speak up!"

I squared my shoulders and spoke rapidly in the Old Language. Frain would not be able to understand me, but Alys would know that I told only truth. "We came to find water. Then Frain sensed his homeland and had to see it. We were very hungry as well, and foraging all the way. When we came to the top of the pass we saw Shamarra kill Fabron—well, cause him to die. And now she has told Frain to follow her. That is why I called you."

"You should be on your way eastward," said Alys angrily. "If you had kept to your course, Frain would be in no difficulty."

"He would be in grave danger of death from thirst and starvation."

"Huh," said Alys unsympathetically. "There would have been rain soon enough, and a jackrabbit or two. Maeve, you have no business being here, and you know you have none. You are part of a far larger design than anything that ever happened in this puny land of Vale."

I knew it was true, as she had said. I made no excuse; I only nodded. "But is Frain part of the pattern here in Vale," I asked, "or is his destiny at the Source with mine, as I have sensed?"

"Frain is a nuisance," said Alys grimly.

I waited, and in a moment she went on.

"This matter between Shamarra and Tirell is a pattern which will work itself out in its own time and way and with its own justice. As Fabron has met with justice at last, the usurper. Shamarra was as much a tool of destiny as a crafter of that death—Frain should not be involved. It was not only Shamarra who lured him out of Vale. But since, with that eager stupidity of his, he has gone and gotten himself back in again—" The goddess's tone turned hard. "—I am going to have to intervene, since you have summoned me. And I hate to intervene. It makes me testy. Shamarra knows that."

I stole a glance behind me. Frain had settled down beside his father and was stroking the dead man's eyelids to close them. Dair had gone wolf, perhaps to threaten Shamarra should she make herself a monster again. Shamarra had folded her hands and stood very still.

"Shamarra," said Alys with distaste but no wrath, "Frain is not entirely yours. I have work for him."

"He has doomed himself—" Shamarra started.

"Another destiny encompasses that doom. Play out your own play here, and leave him to his, and see. He has been gone from you this long, and he is to leave you again, I say." The voice had taken on a touch of sharp edge. "Go now."

Shamarra nodded, gave a graceful curtsy and rippled away down the mountainside. She grew ghostly, seeming to float in the darkness, then disappeared. Frain stood up and gazed after her.

"He is so much like a child," Alys sighed, "that it is useless to scold him. But you, Maeve!" Her voice jerked me around to face her again. "You are no child."

I stood quite silently. I had lost my fear in resignation.

"Nothing to say for yourself?" asked Alys rather nastily. "Well, be mute, then. With the first rays of tomorrow's sunrise. And you will remain mute until the fern flower is found and plucked. That should speed you on your way. When day comes, tend to the dead man, then turn eastward—and take that bothersome Frain with you!"

Thunder sounded, fire ramped and rained, and a blast of wind came that knocked me to my knees. When I looked up, Alys was gone. The great swan had flown, Frain said. Dair told me that the giant moon had faded into starlight. They pulled me up by the elbows and led me back into the shelter of the twin rocks Kedal and Kedur.

We sat all that night shivering and talking, not for diversion but for vital understanding. Frain told us everything that Shamarra had said, and I told him what Alys had decreed. He seemed drifting, dazed, incoherent, even, after Fabron's death and Shamarra's plotting and my own setback. He ended up telling us, not anything about Fabron or Tirell or Shamarra, but about Kedal and Kedur. Two giant and immortal staghounds who had been insulted, called curs, and turned to stone as a result. Fabron had told him the tale when they first met, he said. As he spoke,

111

his eyes remained dry, but slow, seeping tears ran down the rocks from their blind heads far above.

When dawn came we built a cairn over Fabron and left him. No one would ever find him, Frain said. No one came to the mountains except the foolhardy and the most daring of heroes. We trudged back up the steep and rocky slope to the pass, out of the shadow of Lorc Tutosel, the mountains of the night bird. I faced the morning sun. Frain looked back on the far hazy hills of Vale, then down at the cliffs that fell away at our feet, and abruptly he came out of his numbness into anguish.

"Maeve, what in the name of misery am I to do?" he cried, hurling the words out to the heedless wind. "Such a fool I am, I have given my life away to folly—it is not she that I love, she is a stranger, I hardly know her, I detest her, she has betrayed me like all the rest—and yet I love her still! How can that be?" He turned to me fiercely, willing me to understand what he did not. "How has she made such an ass of me? No, it is worse than that; I have done it to myself. I and that lake and an ideal. Look, world, here we see Frain, the noble, loving and faithful one—faithful to what? A witch, a harpy? Ai, I feel like giving my body to yonder void."

I opened my mouth to protest, but no sound came. The muteness had struck. Desolation filled me.

"I can do nothing right," Frain ranted, not looking at me. "I should be speeding to Tirell to warn him, help him, no matter what the goddess says—but I would not be able to face him. I am frightened at the very thought of it, as I was when I saw Fabron. I am such a coward—"

He was talking nonsense, as usual, and I could not tell him so. It is a hard thing not to be able to speak one's mind. I sobbed in anger and self-pity. Frain spun around to peer at me, and his face crumpled.

"And you cannot even speak to me to scold me," he whispered. "And that is my fault as well. Maeve, I am so sorry—"

That was worse than his ranting. I stamped my foot at him, furious at him and at my own sniveling. He grew suddenly very calm, smiling at me oddly.

"Well," he remarked, "it can hardly be said any longer that I go to the Source to learn to speak to Shamarra."

I forgot my tears and watched him warily. The cliff fell away jagged below. Dair stepped to his other side, taut

112

and alert as well. We should have known better. There was always more to Frain than we expected.

"But I am going nevertheless, Maeve Mother," he said almost jauntily. "And I am going to see that you get that flower if I have to find it for you myself. If it takes another eight years. From one madness to the next I flit. So off to the Source we go. Yo ho."

He moved morosely down the shelving rock, and we followed meekly.

From that day on, by some odd shift of fate or will, Frain became our leader, and he felt it. He grew keen as a hound on a faint scent. He seldom slept, and when he did doze he would awaken himself shouting from vivid dreams. Mostly he paced the nights away, his face lean and questing. He did not mention Shamarra again, or the goings-on in Vale; whatever his feelings were in that regard, he kept them very much to himself. He walked steadily, following the straight tug of the Source as surely as I had, and he never led us astray.

He took us down the way we had come and then eastward along the scarp of the Lorc Tutosel with the desert to our right, too close for comfort. Vultures flew there; they reminded me unpleasantly of the Luoni. We found water and food when we needed it in the hollows of the mountains, but just barely enough; we were never really satisfied. The goddess was being severe with us, I could tell.

We made an odd trio, we travelers. Frain could talk to either of us, but for the most part he kept silence. Dair could talk only to me, and I could talk to no one, but I could understand, whereas Frain could understand nothing, and Dair had no one to listen to but Frain. And we were thin and brown and tangled of hair; I no longer looked much like a respectable matron. And we limped from the constant walking; we were all cripples and all mutes and all fools, one way or another. Sometimes, for no reason, I laughed. I could still laugh, much as Dair, in his way, could sing. He sang sometimes at night to amuse us, the notes glassy clear, smooth and sliding, with no cozy human quality about them at all. Once as he sang the wolves of the mountains joined in, each on its own key of wild harmony, and as soon as Dair changed pitch they all did, sliding to a new note with a delicate quaver and a dying fall at the end.

That's all they accept me for, Dair said. *The singing.*

113

I doubted if anyone would have wanted any of us for anything except oddities. Even the slavers would have thought twice about taking us by now, I believed. But there were no slavers about, not on the edge of the desert. And when the barren expanse of sand blocked our way again we struck out across it with an absurd and mindless willingness and a total lack of supplies.

She has made ninnies of us, I thought.

It was hot, too, far hotter than before. The sand burned our bare feet—we had all abandoned our footgear by then, it was worn to pieces. But the way was not long. Only a few days after we started across that wasteland we spied the most unexpected sort of haven, a line of bright green ahead. And as we drew nearer we saw a shine of silver. Not until we stood on the very verge could we believe. A great sheet of water, a magnificent river, bubbled up from the sand at that spot and flowed away between banks of verdant reeds. One foot on sand and the other in marshland, we stood and blinked at each other.

"I declare," said Frain in a startled way, staring at the water that lapped at his instep.

I was more forthcoming. I fell right into the river and drank. The water was fresh and sweet, sand-filtered, and very clear. It seemed to me at the time the best I had ever tasted. Dair drank as well, then whooped and splashed me, capering. Frain still stood bemused. He turned and looked behind him to where the Lorc Tutosel still showed tiny and serrated on the far horizon.

"I declare, it must be where the Chardri comes up again, the great river, after it tumbles beneath the mountains down the south abyss."

I did not know and I did not care. The river, whatever river it was, ran south and east, more east than south for the time, and we followed it. We found wild asparagus and duck eggs and ate them ravenously; even Dair ate the greens. Then we went on. After a while bushes grew along the shore as well as reeds, and then dwarf willows, and then tall sycamore trees, real trees. In their gently shifting shade, half over the water, stood an odd stilt-legged sort of house.

A house!

We froze like startled deer and stared at it, half inclined to flee, as if we had forgotten we were human. The people within were as uncertain as we. Shy brown faces peeped out at us from between reed window slats. Frain collected himself and stepped forward, his one good hand raised to signify peaceful intent.

"Please," he said in Traderstongue, "we are very hungry," and he extended the hand with palm raised, the beggar's gesture of appeal. He could never have been taken for a beggar. His bearing was princely in spite of his rags. But the people understood nevertheless, and silently and hesitantly they issued forth, small muscular men and wide-eyed children and women with their hands half hiding their faces, and they took us in.

They fed us some sort of pudding and great flakes of white poached fish, and then we slept on reed mats that they unrolled for us on the floor. It was good to be back among humans again, very good, even though we were strangers among them and felt it, even though they whispered among themselves and stared at us constantly. The next day they sent us on our way with gifts of fish and wild rice. We stayed that night in another such house, and the next in another. These people lived all along the river. They were gentle folk, almond brown of skin with large dark eyes; their merry round-faced children swarmed through the small dwellings like puppies. We were sorry to leave them, but when the river turned more south than east we saw that we would have to. Our decision caused them great consternation and much high-pitched talk which of course we could not understand.

"You go east?" an old man demanded of us in a dialect we could comprehend, though barely. We nodded. Indeed, we had to go east.

"You three, you woman and wild man and man with withered arm." He pointed at us each in turn. "Legends say end of world is to come when you go east."

We looked at each other and shrugged, thinking we could not have understood him correctly; then we raised hands in farewell and took our leave. They let us go amid much wailing, for they were peaceable folk and would not have known how to stop us.

Once again we were on our own. The land away from the river was no longer desert, but a sort of sandy grassland. The sun shone down with passionate warmth, and birds were mating and singing everywhere. Spring had come, the season of love. Frain did not speak anymore of love, but a poet's paradise of love stretched all around us, doves and deer with their young dappled fawns at their soft flanks and lovely creatures of every kind. I wondered

115

why the river people seemed so afraid, seemed never to come out on this rich grassland. I realized later that it was because we were nearing the holy place.

Near seemed as far as ever to us; we walked for weeks. After a while we noticed marshy patches in the plain. Swarms of stinging insects came up from them and attacked us, rather as if they were guarding the hidden place. Once we reached the true fen, though, they troubled us no more.

That wetland, the most marvelous of fens. We traveled through it for miles and days, our wonder deepening and widening as it did. The spring-green sedges, gathering sand around their roots into hillocks and letting smooth water through in a mazy way between. And waterfowl everywhere, and the white wading birds always standing, and the white water lilies where the shallows deepened into pools. Then islands lush with plumy trees, and the waterways between them golden from the sand beneath and mirroring sky and shadow, meandering, lined with the yellow blossoms of mallow, snakes and turtles sunning themselves on the banks—

Great red fish flickered beneath the ripples, quite tame. "They look as if a person with two hands could practically pick one up," said Frain.

It was not so easy. I tried. Then we tried catching them in Dair's shirt, and that worked no better. Then Frain cut a six-foot shaft from one of the nodding island trees and tied his knife to the end of it and tried to spear them for us. He stood motionless, biding his time, then let loose a mighty thrust. But he missed his aim, and the knife buried itself in the sandy bottom somewhere; the lashings broke.

"Marvelous," declared Frain sourly, searching for it.

Dair had been watching hungrily. Frustration nudged him into change, and in a moment he was a bear, a great lumbering bear with gray-tipped fur, and he slapped fish out of the water for us with nimble paws. We cheered and roasted them and ate; they were delicious. But Frain never found his iron knife, the knife Shamarra had given him years before. And it occurred to me that I had lost something as well. I had not changed form or felt the call of the moon since I had summoned Alys, since I had become mute. All eloquence had left me.

I was content, just the same. Our way led through fascination. Sun and shadow and islets and wandering water-

116

ways and the high arch of greenery overhead and shifting light. We found mossy stepping stones across shallows, and walkways and crannogs built of stone amid the deeper pools; who had made them, when? Elves, I could only think, the elder folk, millennia past. No men lived here, or had ever lived here, for this was a forbidden place. Deer and rabbits and squirrels gazed at us from the thickets unafraid. A hush lay everywhere, broken only by the ripple of water and the calling of birds. It seemed quite right to me that I was mute.

One day at the height of spring we came out from under a canopy of cypress to find that it was the last one. A vast lake spread before us, a freshwater ocean. And from out the midst of the lake rose a mountain. It was shaped more like a vast pillar than a mountain, pearly white in color, its sides nearly vertical, its apex hidden in cloud and a silvery cataract streaming down its nearer side. A bright plume of spray went up where the waterfall met the lake, and there were other such plumes rising all around the base of the great alabaster rock from other waterfalls; their steams spiraled up to the cloud above, lambent in the sunlight. There were bits of rainbow everywhere. We all stood openmouthed, staring. The mountain was enormous, and it stood miles away from us across the open water.

"It is the Source," Frain whispered.

I nodded. It had to be.

INTERLUDE II
from The Book of Suns

Do you remember the Source, People of Peace?

We remember we left it in sorrow.

Do you remember the Day at the Beginning of days?

Our father Adaoun remembers.

Do you remember the Song, Elder Folk, when the One sang out the Source?

We came but a moment later.

The unicorn song. The mountain pushed forth, horn of earth, singular and perfect. You cannot remember, for that was first. No ears heard that song, not even yours.

Sing it for us.

I cannot. I sang seasons, and sky, stars and sun and

117

moon, rainbow, thunder, light, mist. I sang trees, ivy, mistletoe, grass. I sang birds, gave them voice, I sang scampering lizards and squirrels, creatures larger than those, insects, dragons, deer, all that is air and breathes, all that is fearsome—

Sing again!

I cannot. Songs of power can be sung but once and once more—at the end.

The end?

Oneness that was will return from the reaches. Dream of the wanderer on that far shore, the fair white form of single horn. . . . Do you recall, Fair Folk, how oneness was lost?

To men.

My poor creatures of passion. Elves, tell me.

We remember, remember. We are very old. We know the birds flew, the trees were tall, the waters ran pure, there was enough for all to eat and then as our numbers grew still enough and more—

Then men, filled with love and fear.

Passionsong. Mighty One, why did you utter it?

I wanted their heartslove, which you cannot give me.

We saw only fear in men. Why did they fear us? They backed away from us whenever they met us, hid their young from us, confined within walls. They bred beyond reason, grew crowded and restless. They looked outward, wondering what lay beyond the mist—

Very just. The world was put there to know.

We tried hard to help them. We cut them the pathway, hastily, in mere years, since they were impatient. Some went. But they always came back, the place drew them. In passing of seasons they forgot how to speak with us. They threw stones and shouted, called us evil and heartless. They hunted the creatures and killed them for food.

That is their right.

Yes, but how can they stand it? You speak of their love, but we never saw it. They hardened their so-called hearts. They tried to kill us.

Only the cowards tried that.

There were cowards aplenty. All that they wanted was to cut the trees, hunt the birds, harrow the land. We prevented them from it and then they attacked us.

With knives?

With clubs and bows and knives. We learned quickly, we learned bloodshed that day. We used clubs and our own knives and drove them away, threw them down from the high walls, they fell to their deaths who were not dead already—

Then you left as well.

We were sickened and sad, we could not bear to stay. You helped us.

I placed the guardian.

Yes. It comforts us that all the fair things remain there under the eye of the watcher who will not sleep, even though we are absent. . . .

You wandered for many a year.

Seven ages. Far, far from men, somewhere, there would be a place we could dwell in peace, we thought, but we have not found it, for the humans are everywhere. Tell us, Aene, may we never return to the Source?

Perhaps, at the very end. Where will you go till then, Fair Folk?

To the place you have told us of, the unlit land. To the island where wild swans fly, the farthest strand.

book three
FRAIN

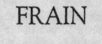

Chapter One

I am Frain, speaking to you from the swanlands beyond. I was a wanderer when I lived in the sunlit lands; I made my way from Vale to the coastline and from the snowladen northlands to the tin mines of Tokar to the tamarind forests of the south. I met many friends and dangers, suffered much and learned much. But I carried my own darkness with me everywhere, no matter how I tried to leave it behind, and I learned nothing that could help me until I met Dair and Trevyn and Maeve.

I was under the black wing by the time I reached Isle— so much so that I did not care any longer what happened to me. It all comes of trying to be noble. Well, I had been so of necessity for Tirell, all my life, he needed me so— and when he came into his own I continued to be noble for Shamarra, who needed me not at all. Old habits are hard to break. So off I went—I can tell you now why I was so frightened of Dair. It was because his marvelous eyes were the eyes of truth on me, and there was so much that I wanted to hide. All the things that were not noble— the pettiness, the jealousy, the angers, all the squelched things I could not abide about myself. Odd; I cannot recall that I did a single noble thing during the time of all that hiding.

Dair hid nothing. He was all honesty, he was most thoroughly and utterly himself. And the beauty of him, this ensorcelled prince with the regal face and the body women swooned over even though he could not be bothered to keep it clean—there's the jealousy again, and a sniffle of self-pity: poor crippled thing, I! Now I can see it, but then I had to be taken by surprise to see anything clearly, and Dair surprised me constantly. He startled love out of me, the rogue. He was so good to me—and Trevyn, True King. I would have stood in awe of him if it were not that I felt as if I had known him all my life. I would look at him and dream of my brother. Tirell could converse with dragons, face their yellow eyes and speak with them mind to mind, and he was a visionary. But I talk too much about Tirell; I always have since I left Vale.

So then there was Maeve, the moon woman, she who roamed the night in form of cat or wolf and who smoothed her hair with prim hands by day. By the time we reached her, Dair had me well in hand. I had been shocked into reluctant acceptance of almost anything except myself— that came later. Maeve mothered me and taught me. And if her son was supremely himself, she was the unity of opposite selves, of many selves, the Maeves of night and day. Talk of the One made more sense to me after I had met her.

"This Source of yours," I asked her one twilight as we walked, "will it be a sort of paradise?"

"What do you mean by paradise?"

There she went again, turning the question back on me. The worst of it was, I seldom knew exactly what I meant.

"Well—no hunger, no danger or enemies, no need to labor. . . ."

"I doubt if it will be like that," she said. "The One made it, and Aene would not have sung something with so much negation in it."

"What is this One?" I burst out with a degree of frustration. It was a god I had never heard of.

"Aene is hunter and hunted, the stag and the serpent," she said. "Aene is rising sun and setting sun and changing moon, all phases including the dark, the sable moon. Aene is day and night, wholeness, abundance of life. There will be nothing lacking in the One's creation."

"You mean there will be danger even there?" I asked in dismay. I very much wanted to rest.

"I dare say. Danger and death are part of the pattern. What is life without death?"

What, indeed? I had gone looking for death myself. It was release, blessed freedom from the paltry, sniveling self. It was union with whatever was. . . . Why, then, was I suddenly so badly frightened?

Dair in wolf form pressed against me. He always felt my fear. I stroked the fur of his back to reassure myself.

If truth be told, I was frightened every step of the way. Not that I made a timid traveler, usually—but this was a journey of a different sort. At first Maeve badgered and coaxed me along toward her Source by force of will and persuasion. Later, at the desert, I came to believe she needed me and I would not leave her. Here, at last, was a chance to be noble! I spoiled it soon afterward and brought the wrath of Alys down on her. Finally, we reached a point where I could feel the tidal tug of the Source for myself.

That was after we encountered Shamarra, of course. It was when I faced Shamarra over the body of my dead father that a small measure of truth came to me and I realized I was a fool. Fate's fool or Shamarra's fool, it scarcely mattered; there would be no escape for me. I was doomed to be forever and always just my stupid self. And there was nothing noble about it, and nothing noble about my feelings for Tirell either. When we walked away from that place truth rode uneasily in me, like something indigestible in my gut. I kept it hidden, like my other hidden shames. But I felt it growing and growing in me, uncomfortably, as if I were pregnant, I, the virgin. And the search for the Source became my own. The Source was my only hope—for what? I scarcely knew. I only knew that any other way lay the black wing of Morrghu.

The call of the Source was like the call of love, like the remembered power of healing moving through me, like a shining sword, like yearning and wanderlust except that it was a focused thing, a painfully focused thing. Only one place in the world would satisfy it. When we reached the great inland sea and looked out to the midst of it and saw that bright, insuperable peak, I smiled.

"Dair?" I asked. "Maeve?"

She looked pale and old in a way that did not suit her. I hated the goddess for what she had done to her, but of course I could not say that. Maeve pointed, and Dair gave that lordly nod of his.

"All right," I said. "Here we go."

We left our packs—well, what was the use of them any longer? We gave ourselves to the lake as we had given ourselves to the desert, wading in without a second thought, without even a staff to feel the way. We waded through that day. We could not lie down and sleep, of course; we waded through the night, the mountain shimmering before us, draped in a sort of luminous haze. It reminded me of Shamarra, a thought I scarcely admitted even to myself.

And through most of the next day we waded, and in all that time the water never rose above our shoulders. Sometime on toward evening we came out and collapsed on the narrow beach. No more than a yard wide, it was nothing but the talus, the rocky debris that fell from the sheer cliffs above. In spite of the discomfort—and it was very jagged rock, indeed—we slept.

"Well," I said to Maeve in the morning, "here we are at your Source. Now that we have found it, what are we to do with it?"

She could not answer, of course. And she knew it was my Source as much as hers by that time. She sat smiling with just the corners of her mouth. Dair said something which of course I could not understand. What a hopeless lot we were.

"Well," I said, "there must be some way in, or up, or whatever." I got up and limped off to the left simply because I happened to be at that end of the line. The rock cut my feet at every step. Before I got far a small stone, hurled at me, stung my back, and I turned to see Maeve pointing imperiously in the opposite direction.

"Now what—" I wondered. Of course. The witch did not want to circle the place widdershins. We set off in the opposite direction with me trailing along in the rear.

The way was long and difficult over the jumbled, sharp-edged rocks. We soon left the narrow beach for the water with its soft, sandy bottom, but then we grew afraid that we would miss something on shore, some hidden entrance or sign of one. So we backtracked and I went ashore, still trying to be noble. Dair ousted me when I started to limp badly, and he took that duty for a while, and then Maeve. The going was slow. By noon we had scarcely left sight of our starting point.

We came to a waterfall, sighting it by its plume of spray long before we reached it. Maeve beckoned, and Dair and I rushed in to shore in great excitement. The waterfalls were such lovely things, we knew they had to be important. But as it turned out, all Maeve had found was food. The stones around the cataract were worn smooth, and in the tumblehole, the hollow at its base, shellfish clung. We sat in the spray, soaking our sore feet, pried them loose with the aid of sharp rocks and ate them raw. More each day I felt like an animal. What was I doing in this wild place? Oh, yes, the Source.

"There *has* to be a way in," I lectured, trying to con-

125

vince only myself. "Why else would we have been brought here?" Some joke of the goddess, I was thinking, though I did not say it. Neither of the others could respond to me much. Maeve was smiling in dry amusement. Dair only nodded. It was hard sometimes to remember that Dair was not only good and faithful but as shrewd as I. More so, really. He was wise; he had insights I knew nothing of. Yet I thought of him as a pet because he could not talk— well, no. Because I could not understand.

We went on. We camped that night with no fuel for a fire, no way to cook the few fish we had caught. Dair ate his raw, but my stomach would not let me since I was no longer utterly starving. Maeve just sat. Since we were no longer totally exhausted, either, we found that we could not sleep on the rocky beach. We sat against the smoother stone of the cliff, quite silent. There was no way we could talk unless I were to hold forth in a monologue, and Dair evidently was not in the mood to sing. It was a lonely night. There was nothing to see, even though the moon was up, nothing except faintly silvershining water that reminded me of my own folly, of Shamarra.

We went on in much the same way the next day, and the next. I lived on shellfish and waterweed and grew tired enough to sleep a little between the watches of the night. I was numb with hardship and with the grief I had kept to myself—oh, so noble of me, to so bravely face my father's death—and with a sort of fatigue of the soul. Still, I was always aware of the splendor of the place, the sheer, stark grandeur of it, white stone that changed in changing light, changing sky and freshwater sea. Lovely—and I sensed yet greater loveliness to come, if only we could find the way.

Chapter Two

It came to me in a dream, how it would be. The sun in my dream was a great golden swan with wings outspread, flared and fanned into a semicircular shape so that the swan was an orb resting on the horizon; it was a sunrise swan. I had never dreamed such a thing before. Everyone in Vale knew that the sun was the great god Aftalun, he who comprised both life and death, rising up and going down. Still, the swan is the true form of the immortal—that might have been Aftalun in swan form.

Be that as it may, I awoke from the dream quite unreasonably certain where the entrance would be. It would lie due east—of course; where else? Just at the opposite extreme of the way we had come. All instinct told me I was right. Had we not been following the sunrise since the day we set out on this quest? We would follow it awhile longer. I said as much to Dair and Maeve.

"So there is no need to be slicing our feet on these rocks any longer," I told them. "We will take to the water. Otherwise we are not likely to find strength to reach the other side."

I was expecting argument—mute resistance, that is to say. But there was none. They followed me without question, and for some several days after that we waded along the shoreline, well away from the rocks. The water must have been very pure, might have had some curative power, even, for our feet healed rapidly. We could never have managed the circuit if we had tried to keep to shore.

Finally came the day when the light of the rising sun shone full and square on the rock face behind our resting backs. We nodded at each other and kept to shore by turns that day to see what we could find.

The discovery went to Maeve, as was only just. She waved us eagerly in to shore, and there it was—just the roughest kind of stairway hewn out of the stone, nothing more than footholds, really. It went up and up, not spiraling around the mountain pillar—for we would have seen it before if it had done that—but weaving back and forth, above and above itself. It was very steep.

We waited out the rest of that day, catching ourselves fish and shellfish, eating nervously, drinking as much as we were able—for we had no flasks anymore, nothing at all really except the few tattered pieces of clothing on our bodies. We spent the night restlessly, and once again I had a strange dream. There were two swans this time, the golden one and another that was white, or argent, silver, both of them in a vast starless sky of midnight blue, and they flew toward each other and embraced, their wings intertwined, turning, turning in air—and they made one sphere; how could that be? Then I saw the moon nestled into the arms of the sun. . . .

I awoke, looking for the sun, then dozed again. At the first hint of dawn we were all up. And as soon as it was light enough to see we started.

Maeve went first. It was only fair that she should go first. I came behind her, then Dair behind me—to help me if I should falter, I sensed. Insulted pride stirred sluggishly in me, then subsided. Who was I to be proud?

We climbed. All day we climbed. I wondered at first what primal folk it was who had made these steps, time out of mind, the Beginning time thousands of years before. Maeve might have been able to tell me if she could speak—I stopped wondering as we climbed higher. When my good arm was toward the mountainside, the sheer stone, I was all right; even the most illusory of fingerholds gave me confidence. But when the way doubled back and my crippled arm lay toward the wall, I sweated and trembled and could not look down. I did not dare look up, not ever. I could not bear to think how far we had to go.

Dear goddess, all gods, all powers, mighty One, please let us not be caught by nightfall. . . .

If the climb went all the way to the top we would be, surely, even though we had started at dawn. I tried not to think of clinging to the rock all night or feeling my way up it in the dark. . . . The mountain seemed to push against us from above, threatening to topple us out into the void. We were all far too preoccupied to notice hunger and thirst. Our mouths were dry from more than thirst. I could hear Maeve wheezing ahead of me, and on the turns I caught glimpses of her face, strained and white. I knew mine looked no better. I felt half sick, afraid I would disgrace myself and vomit or cry, and then too frightened to worry about disgrace. We were more than halfway, surely we had to be, but we climbed in deepening shadow, dusk had started to fall.

And then there was a sort of slot instead of the everlasting steps. We had to crawl along it, quite level but still ever so close to the edge—and then there was a waterfall, just as we had known there must be. A veil of rushing water stood between us and the clutching air—we were behind the cascade. It offered no substantial protection, I knew, but it looked so solid that I felt immensely comforted. And then the cave, behind the waterfall, just as I had pictured it in my mind, wide and high and blissfully solid underfoot. Shakily I stood up, Maeve and Dair stood up on either side of me, we all smiled crazily at each other, absurdly happy. We were alive! We did not care what happened next, if we starved in that place or were killed or what. We grinned at each other, stretched and sat down to rest.

"What is that?" I muttered, peering and squinting in the uncertain light.

Farther back in the cave, a glint like that of old gold, muted in the gloom, unmoving. As our eyes grew accustomed to the dimness we saw that it was a griffin, sitting and looking at us. We were too spent to react to it much; we merely sat. I had never seen a griffin before, but Fabron had crafted them many times on silver or gold cups or cauldrons or clasps, so I knew a live griffin when I saw one. It had no wings. It sat on its furred haunches and fixed its eagle eyes on us with no hint of threat or anger; the great downcurved beak and the long leonine tail remained still. It waited and watched and never moved.

"The guardian," I said. Of course there had to be a guardian, and the griffin made an ideal one, honorable, faithful, courageous, and vengeful if need be. Dair heard me and nodded.

I got up and walked forward a few paces. The griffin clacked its beak and hissed, a gentle but unmistakable warning, and the tufted tip of its tail moved as if it had a life of its own. I went back to the others.

"Can we get past it when it sleeps, do you think?" I asked them.

Maeve shook her head, giving no reason. Well, of course she could give no reason. I looked at her.

"Maeve, do you have any idea what we ought to do?"

She nodded.

"Well, what? Can you make shift to tell us?"

She felt around until she found a loose shard of rock and then started scratching industriously at the cave floor. I squinted to see what she was doing. Paler yet in the pale stone, lines appeared in the forms of strange runic letters. I could read a little in my native tongue—I was no scholar, I was too ungoverned as a boy—but I could not read that. I shook my head. She pointed to Dair.

"Dair, read that?" I knew better. Maeve made the hand signal which is usually taken to indicate an overly talkative mouth.

"Dair is supposed to say that?"

She nodded.

"But what is it?" I glanced at Dair, and he looked back at me with no particular enlightenment in those odd purple eyes of his. Maeve lifted a hand as if in greeting, though to be sure we had all met before. Dair grinned toothily and got to his feet, growled something and ambled over to meet the griffin.

It was the greeting, of course, the old elfin greeting, the *Laifrita thae,* though I knew nothing of it at the time. All that was necessary was for the griffin to be spoken to as a friend in that ancient tongue. Dair was a man speaking in the way of wolves, but it was all the same; that language knew no barriers. . . . I did not understand at the time. I stood and watched as Dair and the griffin conversed. Dair gestured toward us, his companions. The griffin bowed its eagle head gravely to hear him, shifted its great talons on the stone. Then quite courteously it rose and moved aside to let us pass.

Us, I thought, full of unreasoning certainty that I was intended to enter. But to the griffin the welcomed ones were really only Dair and Maeve. She could not speak for herself, but she was one of the special few; the griffin knew that simply because Dair had told him so. Dair could not possibly have lied about her, any more than he could lie about me—

Dair saluted and passed, then Maeve with a nod and a smile. I followed her—and the griffin sprang up with a roar, its talons raised and its tail lashing wildly. I stood frozen, afraid to advance, unwilling to flee. But in three long strides Dair came before me, my shield, and Maeve grabbed me and pulled me impatiently after her. Dair confronted the griffin a moment longer and then backed away, unscathed. It could not harm him, or not wittingly, having once given him its safe-conduct. But it let out a great bellow of wrath and frustration. And its tail, switching back and forth in a frenzy, struck him and left a little cut on his arm.

Chapter Three

The passage curved up and up. We felt our way along it, at first standing and later on hands and knees because of the steep ascent, all in raven blackness. But at least we no longer were afraid of falling; we were enclosed, secure. We came out at last onto a level surface that was soft, springy and faintly familiar of scent—I felt I should know that scent but I could not identify it. Nor could I comprehend the rustling darkness all around us. I was confused, but too weary to care. We all lay down where we were, a little distance from the entry, and slept.

Hunger and riotous birdsong awakened us a few hours later, at dawn. The darkness had been nothing more than night, and the soft surface beneath us was moss. We sat up, blinking, bathed in hushed, filtered light. Great monoliths rose all around us. Only after several stunned moments was I able to identify them as trees. They were immense, twice the size of any trees I had ever seen. Even the trees of the Wyrdwood back in Isle were saplings compared to these. Streams of muted, hazy sunlight trickled down through the pinpoint foliage far above. Butterflies swam in the light; from where we sat, at the bottom of it all, they looked tiny, mere jewel flecks. The birds which we heard so clearly could not be seen. They were hidden somewhere amid the great canopy overhead.

We got up and blundered off, staring up and in every direction, scarcely noticing where we were going. All around us there stirred a constant chirp and ripple of life, a quick movement here, a flash of color there—honeybees in the air, and lacewings. Big flowers growing right out of the trunk of a tree, perhaps thirty feet above my head.

Vines looped into a love knot. Great clumps of mistletoe forming their own shiny balls amid the foliage. The chuckle of some strange bird, and the chuckle of water, just ahead—

Each of us broke into a faltering run and stumbled into the stream, sank down and drank. I knew right then that I had reached the paradise of my dreams. The water was more than water; it was substance, essence of life itself. I tasted strength in it, and it was lovely, it ran around me like liquid silk. And what lay under my hand?

Jewels. The streambed was full of gems, all colors, washed round, turning the rippling water into rainbow. We let them lie, for we saw something more valuable— food. Sitting right in the shimmering water, we feasted. Eating was only a matter of reaching up and grasping the nearest fruit, for the smaller shrubs and berry bushes, which could not live in the shadows of the giants, crowded around the waterbed where the sunlight came down suffused by cloud. Pomegranate, loveapple, may, meddlar, sorb, quince, wild currant, fig, woodberry, goldenberry by the fistful, red and yellow fruits I did not know the names of—there was plenty, enough and more than enough, even for the birds. We ate.

There was a sense of coming home, home to the primal home, of release of care, of rocking in the arms of the All-Mother. As if we were at last allowed to be tired, we went off again and slept. Then near evening we ate again. Giant fireflies, the brightest I had ever seen, lit up the dusk like the missing stars. We slept through the night without a thought of quest or danger. My dreams were full of magic and bright colors, but I do not remember them well. Then we woke and ate.

There were ferns everywhere, giant six-foot ferns along the streams, ferns growing right from the bights of the trees, ferns underfoot amid the moss, ferns hanging down from the tangled and hanging vines, feeding on air.

"How are we to know which fern bears the magical flower?" I asked Maeve.

She shook her head in that stolid way of hers. The goddess was to tell her somehow, I supposed. The very thought of the goddess annoyed me. I smothered the feeling.

"You say it blooms only at midnight of Midsummer's Eve?"

She nodded. I felt my stomach knot.

"But—when is Midsummer's Eve?" I had kept no track of time, amid all our exertions, and I didn't see how she could have, either.

She had not. She shrugged. I turned away, flinging up my one good hand in despair. Dair grinned at me. His grin was most aggravating, though perhaps he did not intend it that way.

"Come on," I ordered, and stomped off.

We went exploring. We went to the edge first, where the stream cut its way through the surrounding rock and became waterfall, giving itself to the void. We looked out through the gap into nothing more than mist, a soft, luminous veil of cloud and spray. Cloud nourished the great forest, bedewed the leaves, let light in only gently, here so close to the scorching sun. Mountain cradled us and cloud was the coverlet.

We walked along the edge for a while, studying the great alabaster rocks that bounded the mountaintop cloud forest. Ferns grew on them, too, and columbine, and snails the size of my fist crawled amid the flowers, their shells as ornate as Fabron's finest smithwork. We walked for a day and passed two more waterfalls, two more streams, they came out from—somewhere—like spokes of a giant wheel. There were gems in each streambed, and again we let them lie. They seemed no more precious to us than the other marvels of this place. We walked amid wonder. Then we slept and turned toward the unknown center, the Very Source.

There was a kind of bird, a round, comical-looking bird about the size of a dove, pied green and tan and gold like a harlequin. It was very tame. It lived near the streams and grinned at us from shrubs as we went by. It had a wide beak that ended in a smirk, so wide that when it opened its mouth it seemed to split its head in half. The sound that came out of it was like a hooting laugh. I called it the hootoo bird, or sometimes, to insult it, I called it froggyface. Maeve smiled and called it nothing at all. What Dair called it I do not know. We followed the stream back to the Source, and the hootoos smirked at us all the way.

It took two days. I felt the tug all the time, like a throbbing ache in my heart, not at all unpleasant, the ache of love. It was sometime during that walk that I noticed the sore on Dair's arm. The cut the griffin had given him was not healing—it was open and festering. Odd, that in this place where everything was so clean and fresh, dew-bathed, such a thing could happen. I made Dair bathe it in stream water, puzzled; he had been in and out of streams often enough since we had come to this place and he was far cleaner than was his wont. And there was a balm in the water, too; I could feel it. Why had it not helped him?

Either he or Maeve might have known the truth about the spine hidden in the tuft of hair at the end of the griffin's leonine tail, about the poison. But of course they could not tell me. Perhaps they would not have told me anyway. They were always protecting me.

Dair was as strong as a bear, stronger than any man I had ever met, stronger even than Tirell, I told myself. He would soon be better, I thought.

We were getting very near. I could tell. The tug—it moved me to tears I could not understand, tears I had to suppress. Memories of times—long before I was born? How could that be? How could this place I had never seen be the home of my heart? But I felt that, and I could tell that Maeve felt something of the sort as well. She looked up, taut, expectant. The canopy of forest giants was coming to an end. Tree ferns nodded over us, uncurling spiral heads. We stepped through and saw—

"Oh, Mother Adalis," I breathed.

Maeve said nothing at all, her eyes shining. Dair made a sound, and I knew without question that he invoked something, too—the god of wolves? It was deity, and it was the Tree of all trees.

It towered above the great moss-bearded oaks behind us as they towered over us. Its trunk was the breadth of a castle and its crown disappeared in cloud; acres of ground lay beneath its spreading boughs. It was a world, a dwelling, a home and a marvel unto itself; it supported forests on its branches; trees grew there, feeding on the rich mold of its upper bark; they looked small, but they were as large as any normal tree in Vale or Isle. A house could have been built on any one of those boughs. And the water—it was the gift of the Tree, it flowed from the seams of the trunk itself, cascading down and forming its several streams and flowing away in every direction of the ringing horizon.

"Mother Adalis," I whispered again. "That must send its taproot down to the very fundament of earth, to the flood beneath."

Maeve nodded. It was the World Tree.

We walked slowly nearer, step by hesitant step, gawking. All was in a hush, not silence exactly but silken texture of soft sound, trickle of water and swish of wings—giant dragonflies flew over the many waters, jewelglowing, iridescent; their six-foot wingspan looked small beneath the splendor above them. Lush, deep grass grew underfoot, and the most intricate of ferns, and dense thickets of goldenberry clustered at random amid the grass and ferns and between the streams. I disturbed a great snake resting in the grass. It slid away and flowed into the nearest stream and swam off, not bothering to harm me. There were quail nesting in the grass also. But something drew me besides plenty and magnificence and the cleansing marvel that is water—

"The Tree," I murmured with sudden certainty. "It is all made of living metal, the very marrow of earth; it is pure iron. I can feel it right down to my bones."

Maeve glanced at me intently. Dair made a questioning sound. I gestured earnestly at them.

"Folks say smiths have molten metal for blood," I told them. "That Tree is the lodestone that drew me here. Come and see." I strode with insane temerity straight up to the trunk that loomed like a wall before me.

It was true. The bark was yielding, cushiony, but nevertheless metal—spun iron, like foundry bloom. Its color was a dully glimmering dark gray. The substance beneath it was as hard as cast iron, hammered iron or steel. The leaves rustled far above. What they were we could not tell, but there was a golden glint to them—or perhaps that was only the evening light. Night was near.

"What now?" I asked, suddenly abashed by my own boldness. "Do you think we dare stay here?"

Maeve sat down on the thick green grass, looking quite serene, and that gave us the answer. We would wait for a sign.

Chapter Four

We stayed for some days, eating the many fruits of the streambanks and the meadow. There were trumpet-shaped vineflowers all around the gigantic roots of the Tree, and each of them gave forth a drop of pure, thick honey every morning. We sucked them greedily. We grew lazy, in fact, scarcely bothering to catch the swift fish of the streams or make a fire to cook them on. But as for staying there, we had no choice but to await the goddess's pleasure—or wrath. And for all my watching, I could not pinpoint sunrise or sunset through the misty veil of cloud or count the hours between. It seemed to me that the days were still lengthening, but I could not be sure. Midsummer's Eve might already have passed, unbeknownst to us. And not a sign of a flower did I ever see on any fern.

Preoccupied as I was with the problem of the fern flower, perhaps I had some excuse—but I am ashamed of how long it took me to see that Dair was sickening. It came to me at dusk one day when I saw a flash of white tail in a thicket, a rabbit, and I realized that Dair had not eaten any meat in—weeks? Since we had left the wetlands? And when had he taken to wearing the shirt that usually hung like a rag from his waist?

"Why do you never hunt anymore?" I asked him.

He shrugged. Only one shoulder moved—the left arm hung stiffly by his side. I was all too familiar with that unbalanced gesture in myself. One stride took me to him, and he edged away from me, grumbling.

"Let me see," I said.

He started to amble away, pretending not to hear me. I hurried after him and caught him by the shoulder.

137

"Let me see that arm!"

He tried to shake me off, and I clung to him. I was growing frantic. We tussled—any other time I would not have dreamed of challenging him, but it seemed we were evenly matched now, and that fact made me more panicky than ever. He was as one-armed as I. We tripped each other and ended up rolling and wrestling on the ground, no very friendly contest. I panted and Dair snarled, threatening to bite. I caught at his sore arm, still intent on looking at it, and the snarl turned to a yelp of pain. I could have wept for contrition.

"Dair, *please*," I begged.

Then I realized I was playing the fool again, fighting him for nothing—it was too dark for me to see anything by then. I got up and left him, cursing and trying not to cry. And, the perversity of him, he came after me.

"In the morning," I told him. "Promise me." And of course I could not understand what he said in reply.

It must have been a promise. In the morning he was there and he let me look at the arm. The black fist of fear gripped me at the first glimpse of it. The sore itself had not spread, but the arm was pasty white and useless, bloated, paralyzed, the skin cracking open bloodlessly. Dair's fingers felt like sausages in mine, nothing more. I met his eyes, stricken.

"Name of the Almighty, Dair, what contagion is this?" I stammered.

He could only look back at me. The eyes of truth on me—I could not face them. I turned to Maeve, and she winced away as I had, biting her lip. It struck me that she looked not much better than Dair—too pale, far too thin. Why? Had she come to her Source only to die? My mind whirled.

"I wish one of you could talk to me," I whispered. I felt as helpless as an infant, but I struggled against the feeling.

"There has to be something I can do," I said stubbornly. "A poultice, a potion—something has to help."

I brought gemmy mud from the streambank and plastered it on Dair's arm, hoping vaguely that the muck would draw something unclean out of him—I was not skilled in this sort of healing, and I knew it, to my dismay. Dair tolerated my attentions much as all men suffer fools: not gladly. When I came at him later that day with a mash

I had made out of mushrooms he muttered ungraciously and shuffled away.

Within a few days, though, he was too weak and listless to evade me. I watched him with ever-increasing alarm, forgetting all about the fern flower. I could see that he was having trouble moving around. Then he stopped trying altogether; he sat or lay near the World Tree through the days, and he stopped eating as well. I brought him fruit, honeyflowers, even grubs and snails and some of the other horrid things I knew he liked. At first he would turn away his head. Later, though he still did not eat, he would accept the stuff from me with a docility that sent chills to my spine. I had never seen him so tame. He did not have the strength even to growl at me.

I tried every way I could think of to help him. I mixed every kind of drink I could devise, short of poison, and begged or badgered him into trying them all. I made poultices out of all sorts of odd and barbaric things. The contagion, whatever it was, had moved from his arm through most of the rest of him; his limbs were as useless as so many sticks of wood. I tried to rub his stiffened body to warm and ease him, but the skin cracked open right under my hands, and his flesh was oozing and yellowish beneath; it was awful. I pounded fruit into mush and tried to make him eat it, tried to force it in between his tightening teeth. He would take water from me, nothing more. As the days crawled by I cooked fish, fungi, moss, ferns, whatever came into my hazy mind for him, without avail.

Maeve probably afforded him more comfort than I did. She would sit by him and hold his head on her lap for hours at a time, stroking his hair and trying not to trouble him. I could not be still. My mind was in a constant broth and boil, in desperate search of a remedy—there had to be a remedy. . . . I often felt Maeve's gaze on me, full of pity and concern. Concern, for me! Her son lay—I would not say dying, I refused to think that. Her son lay terribly ill, and her concern was for me. I felt dismally unworthy, and angry at the same time that she could not talk to me to comfort me.

Dair became shaky. He shivered in the slight chill of night and could not sleep. Maeve and I would lie close on either side of him to warm him. Sometimes, dozing, he moaned. Those small sounds went through me like swords. Here we were at the navel of the world, the very Source of all that was, cradled by ineffable beauty, surrounded by marvels of every sort, every moment a new joy to the senses, flower-scented breeze, pearly rainbow sky, food fit for the gods, sweet music of birdsong, a paradise beyond belief, and—he was wasting away, my friend was—dying before my eyes. . . .

I had not said that, I could not bear to even think it! I pushed the thought far away.

It was the next day that I noticed how labored his breathing was. Paralysis had spread through his limbs and to his organs, and now each breath became a gasping effort. I went through the day with Dair's death looming and looming at the back of my mind, unfaceable, like the thing in the dark inscrutable lake. When I brought him water I noticed that his eyes were the color of purple twilight, unfocused, dim. Or was it only that dusk was indeed falling—

I had not helped him, I had failed him, I had failed him utterly, and I hated to hurt him and fail him again, but I had to try. I steeled myself to try.

"The Tree," I said hoarsely. "The Tree is made of iron. Lay him by the Tree."

Maeve looked at me in mute plea, begging me not to disturb him.

"Lay him by the Tree, I say!"

I tugged at her, and she also must have had her insane hopes, for she helped me. We carried him the little distance to where the massive roots swelled out of the ground, and he groaned but did not cry out. We laid him under the slight overhang of one bulging root, the chill, gray ferrous bark pressed against his belly and side. I knelt by him and laid my forehead against the Tree, against hard, striving muscles of living iron. I closed my eyes and pressed my one good hand to Dair's pallid flesh, trying to think, trying to pray, to call on my god—what god? Some god, any god, goddess, whatever, for healing—there was not a hint of power in me, no healing in me, as I had known quite well there would not be. I could kneel there all night and the end would be the same.

A thought occurred to me. I groped around and found a sharp rock, a white flint—damn it that I had lost my knife, or I would have done better. I sawed away at the wrist of my useless left arm until the blood ran. The accursed crippled thing might be good for something after all, I thought. I hoisted it, dripping, streaming, and laid it on Dair's face and tried to open his mouth to let the drops run in. I felt certain at the time that this would be the remedy at last, but Maeve ran over to me with a gasp of shock, plucking at me in an annoying way, as if I had done something quite untoward.

"He needs red," I explained to her lucidly. He had not eaten meat in so long, was it any wonder that his face was gray? But she tried to pull me away.

One of those smirking birds flew by and gave its hooting laugh, hootoo, hootoo. And quite suddenly I went crazy.

Chapter Five

I struck at the Tree with my flint, struck, stabbed, again and again, with the spongy bark bearing it all quite indifferently. Finally I threw it, hard, at Maeve. She dodged. Methodically, as if it mattered, I began to rip the honeytrumpet flowers from around the Tree. Damn it that I had lost my knife—

"It is not fair!"

I stood still for a moment and shouted the words at the darkening sky.

"It is not fair! Dair is the only one who has ever loved me not to betray me—you cannot take him from me! You cannot!"

I picked up a rock, the biggest one I could heft in my one hand, and flung it, not bothering to watch where it fell. Damn it that I had lost the use of my other arm. With it I would have been able to fling a larger rock. Maeve stood watching me warily.

"They all betrayed me," I choked. "Tirell—" I tried to stop, but there was a torrent of anger in me pressing to be let loose. I had unleashed a trickle and it was fast turning to a flood. Maeve could not ask the questions, say the prodding words, but it did not matter; she had trained me well. She might as well have been speaking to me. I turned from the unresponsive sky and shouted at her.

"The arrogant bastard, he always knew he could treat me like dirt, take me for granted, he didn't care! He—" I paused, panting, and dropped down to claw at the grass. "He drove her away from me, raped her, took her, he—"

I glanced at Maeve, who nodded gravely. It seemed absurdly important that I should make this all perfectly clear.

"He *hit* me!" I cried. "He came at me with that great bludgeoning sword of his and wounded me, broke my shoulder, crippled me for life—and then he got a kingdom for it and a doting bride—and I—"

Pettiness. Self-pity. I didn't care. I plunged on.

"I got only a broken heart. And Fabron, my father, my own father, sold me into slavery, deceived me, lied to me, pretended to be my friend but didn't have the guts to tell me the truth—"

How unfair of me, how ignoble. I didn't care. I felt saliva run down my chin. Or was it tears. No matter. Nothing mattered.

"Made a fool of me in front of Shamarra," I panted. "As if she had not made me fool enough. And that damn Adalis-Alys-whatever the bloody flood her name is—she laughed at me!"

I cursed the goddess by every name of hers that I knew, searching my mind anxiously to make sure I did not forget one. It took some time. After I was done with the goddess I cursed the pantheon of Ascalonia and the sacred kings, Tirell and the whole line of Melior back to Aftalun, one by one. Childish, but it helped just a little. Then I cursed that strange and unknown god who had sung this place, the One, whoever that was. And the earth did not even tremble, though Maeve did.

Then I set about to destroy as much of the paradise as I could. It had no right to be there when Dair lay dying.

Maeve cautiously sat down after a while, watching me. I went about kicking and gouging and snatching with my hand, breathing hard and muttering fervidly to myself, "Let them laugh *now!*" I blundered against fruit trees, broke sticks from them and threw them as hard as I could, shouting wildly. I found a clump of tree ferns and beat and smashed it down to the ground. I stamped and jumped on the vanquished boughs.

"Damn—Shamarra," I shouted between heaving breaths. "Letting me—bathe in that—deathly lake of hers, never telling me—what I was doing. She always—scorned me, laughed at me. She hated me. She—"

Something moved in me and I felt horribly afraid. Maeve was sitting there so quiet, so vulnerable, and Dair lying helpless, and there was a beast loose in the gathering dark; did they not sense it? I did. I gasped in terror, turned and ran.

"She killed my father!" I shrieked to the night.

I was glad that I had lost my knife, lost the use of my arm. I had it in me to stab, slay, kill, I knew that now. The healer had murder in his heart. I myself was the reason I would not face Fabron or Tirell, the reason I had left them. I was the beast in the night. And the face, that hideous face, floated on the surface of the darkness, as if night were a deep and brooding pool.

It seemed quite real, a tangible illusion. It fully convinced me at the time. I thought I could reach out and shatter the water, but I did not dare, boneless hands would drag me down—it was an ugly face, contorted, glaring, frothing at the downstretched mouth—monstrous—it was the face I had seen in Shamarra's lake. Grotesque, fearsome—the face I had given the faceless spirits of the dead.

It was my own.

My very own reflected rage, hidden in every other way, and it sent a long spear of fear through me. I ran from it, whimpering, and it ran with me effortlessly, never leaving me. I could not have been more terrified if there had been a serpent wrapped around me, a demon clinging to my shoulders. "Please—" I begged the night, the face, but they did not answer.

I must have run for hours through the deep of night, the black pit of night, the darkest night I have ever known. No moonlight or starlight could penetrate the veiling cloud of that mountaintop, and the fireflies one by one went to sleep; I was all alone with only my unwelcome self for company, my mirrored self, my dark twin. It chivied me through the forest, hunted me through the thickets and streambeds, harried me as the Luoni harry the departing souls of the untruthful, cutting me off at every desperate turn, driving me toward—what end? I ran blind, crazed, bloody and sweaty and exhausted. At last I blundered into some sort of benighted copse—

I stood rooted, feeling the presence of the face at my back but unable to move. A kind of voiceless singing thrummed through me, a shivering, and I knew that I was in the presence of something holy. I scarcely breathed. I stood in terror and awe.

A glow, a tiny glow in the darkness, like the spark deep in the heart of a ruby, down at my feet, almost hidden in earth. It grew, wavering, flaming, flaring, blood red. It was a cup of honeydew, a mystic grail of flame and blood and tears, it was a head with hair afire, it was the sunswan, flamefeathers, flamepetals, and as it grew it climbed, a small fiery beast, a living thing, as alive as I was—perhaps more so. Up its stalk it climbed until it burned at the level of my face, and in the heartred pulsating liquid light of it I could see the leaves, fern leaves, each one a frost-flake, I thought they would melt before I could move—it was the fern flower, fire flower, Maeve's flower of hope. For Maeve—and without another thought I reached out, grasped the stem and plucked it.

I screamed aloud as I had never screamed before. The forest rang with the sound. I can still hear the echo in my mind.

Glory be to Eala, the pain! Intense, searing, it made my whole body cry out in sympathy with my hand. I felt as if I had snatched a rod of white-hot iron out of the coals of Fabron's forge. Worse—a burning serpent. The stalk writhed and squirmed in my hand as if it were a live adder. I very nearly dropped it in the shock of pain and surprise, but I hung on. And then the true pain struck me.

The pain of truth. The enormity of it, that I should hate my brother whom I loved, my father whom I loved, Shamarra—yet it was so. My own depravity stabbed me like my missing knife, stung worse than the burning thing in my hand. How could I be so—monstrous, so ignoble? I heard all the green things I had hurt crying aloud in pain. Truly. Their small voices sounded right inside my head, making a chorus of lament that matched my own. And the face still leered before me.

I sank down and wept.

HE KILLED MY SEEDMATE.

My love, the purity of my love, lost.

HE HAS TORN OFF MY LIMBS, MY LEAVES.

All my life I had thought of myself as one generous of heart—

HE HAS BROKEN ME, TRAMPLED ME DOWN.

A healer, a chivalrous warrior, the most loyal of followers to my brother—I had been great, in my way. At the very least I had been good. And now all that was gone, it seemed. My heart was full of spleen.

WHY HAS HE HURT US? WHY?

What was I to do, how could I live—

HUSH, the fern flower said. THE SWAN LORD HAS COME AT LAST. LOOK, HE WEEPS.

BUT HOW CAN THAT BE?

THE SWAN LORD, A DESTROYER? IT WAS SAID HE WOULD BE A HEALER—

145

I TELL YOU, IT IS HE. The voice of the fern flower shivered through me, warm.

BUT WHY HAS HE HURT US?

PAIN IS IN THE PATTERN. Oh, the love, the gentle forgiveness in those words. My eyes were closed in agony, but I heard.

HEALING IS FOR WHOLENESS. WAIT AND SEE.

A rustling went through the forest like the stirring of leaves before dawn.

THE SWAN LORD! one soft voice said.

THE SWAN LORD HAS COME! breathed another.

BUT IF IT IS HE—

IT IS HE. That flameflower, that voice like a lover's—

THEN IT IS TRUE WHAT HAS BEEN SAID, THAT THE SEED WILL BE SPREAD.

IT IS TRUE. Words vibrant with joy.

THE MAIDEN GOES TO BRIDEBED!

AT LAST WE WILL BE HEARD!

There was more, a paean of rejoicing, but I remember it only confusedly. Something was happening. The fiery pain in my hand was easing, but that was the least of it. A sense of strong comfort was coming to me. The pattern—I was very tired, and I could not think of the things Maeve had told me. I could think only of a quiet lake, a fair black swan with a reflection of white. Healing is for wholeness. . . . A face floated into view.

I opened my eyes. It was there before me, calm, almost smiling, the face on the surface of the dark. It was—was it really my own freckled visage? But it was beautiful, as beautiful as Dair's! As I gasped it rippled and blurred, fading.

"Wait!" I cried, I wanted to shout, though my voice came out a husky whisper. "Please—" It was awash as if in tears. "Please stay," I begged. It was dark and lovely, and it was me, mine or part of me. In that moment I could not bear to lose it.

I AM NOT GONE, it said gently. I AM IN YOU, FOR YOU HAVE ACCEPTED ME. REST NOW. SLEEP. And it swam away.

Away or within—at once the words comforted me. I lay down on the ground, my face nestled to loamy earth, the fern flower held close to my side, and for a few hours I slept. I remember that sleep as deep and refreshing, and yet it was full of dreams. Voices chanted in my dreams.

146

I dreamed that it was a woman who lay by my side, a woman fair as a flower, all clothed in petals of light. Petals caressed my face, her lips brushed my face, and they burned like fire. "The kiss of the goddess," she said. "You will not always be a virgin, Frain." My tears ran down and mingled with her fire, and the two together made a new and lovely thing. I dreamed again. I saw the midnight swan, the white swan and the golden swan, the sunswan in my dreams, and then I awoke, full of the feeling of blessing. It was just dawn.

Dawn. It had been a rather short and crowded night. The sun comes up early on Midsummer's Day. I got up, blinked in the dewy light and looked at what I held in my hand.

A length of fern, the most delicate of ferns, and on the stem a single flower. I had never seen any flower like it, even amid all the wonders of the Source. It was all the colors of sunflame, crimson and cloud pink and ruddy gold, and it held its petals cupped like sacral hands. The calyx was of copper color, and just at the heart of the flower I saw a fine-veined stain of blood red, so red it looked as if it were moist—perhaps it was. I didn't dare touch.

THE DAYSPRING COMES, sang the wind.

LIFT HIGH YOUR HEADS, flowers told each other. SPREAD YOUR PETALS WIDE.

HEY HOOTOO HOOTOO GOOD DAY! shouted a pied bird.

Sunlight touched the upper leaves of the trees.

"Have I hurt you?" I whispered to the fern flower, speaking in a tongue that was not my own, a far more ancient tongue, the Old Language—it had come to me, and I had hardly noticed amid all the terrors and marvels of the night.

EVERYONE HURTS SOMETHING SOMETIME.

"I am very sorry," I faltered.

BUT WHY? I AM MEANT TO BE YOURS.

Not mine—Maeve's! With a start I plunged off to find her. I had strayed a long way from the Tree. I found a stream and drank from it, then followed it back to the Very Source. It took at least an hour at the best speed I could muster. When I got there at last, Maeve was still sitting where I had left her, leaning against the Tree with Dair's head in her lap. I hurried up and knelt before her.

"Your flower," I said. "Maeve, here is your flower. Look."

She only gazed back at me with a small, glad smile. She didn't move.

"Take it," I urged. "It will let you talk again. Alys said so. Here."

THERE IS NO NEED, she said. She spoke to me as the flower had—her voice sounded right inside my head. That was the way the dragons had talked to Tirell. . . . I stared at her openmouthed.

HELP DAIR, she said.

Dair! He had to be dead. After all the killing I had done, could he still be alive? But he was, his breathing shallow and shaky, his face toadbelly gray.

I thrust the fern flower at Maeve. "Hold that for me," I muttered. I gathered Dair up into my one-armed embrace and pressed us both hard against the mighty metal Tree. Then I waited, feeling as empty as a dry shell on the seashore. My night of rage and anguish had left me purged, but what was to fill me again? Love was not enough.

"Alys," I whispered. "Aftalun."

Dair could not wait long.

"Moon and Sun—"

Wolf and dog, she had said. Night and day. Wholeness. . . . All the Source seemed hushed, breath-holding, even the laughing bird.

"Almighty One!"

The tide rolled in.

The power rushed and surged in me or through me, from far beyond or deep within, from the World Tree, the world, the sky, the flood beneath, drumming, beating, unbearable, my eyes saw only white fire—it was fire, fire and the flood; I can describe it no other way. It was a torment and an ecstasy, as always, as I remembered it from years before, but never so strong before, and so long, never! I thought I would die, and I knew Dair would live, and I forced myself to hold him to the Tree, not to tear away; I was crying like a virgin on her wedding night with pain and joy. Healing, healing power—then it was gone, leaving me drained and weak, as always—though never so weak before—and Dair was sitting up against the Tree, tanned and healthy, looking back at me in bewilderment.

"Dair!" I hugged him with all the feeble strength that was left in me. I never wanted to let go of him. "Dair, you're alive! I thought you were dead—Dair!" I remembered further cause for joy. "Dair, talk to me, say something! I can understand you now, truly I can! We can really talk together after all this time—" I drew back a little to look at him. His mouth was moving soundlessly. He seemed stunned. I glimpsed Maeve off to one side, smiling as broadly as I had ever seen her. I ignored her.

"Dair, would you say something?" I pleaded. "Cat got your tongue?"

Frain, you idiot, haven't you noticed—you're mauling me with both arms!

The twist was gone out of my left shoulder. My left hand rose to greet me. I stared at it, unbelieving, reached over with the other one and touched it, felt firm muscles and flesh. There was a ragged scar on the left wrist, white and healed. There was a white weal across the palm of the right hand where I had held the fern flower, and they told me later there was a small white crescent mark on my face. Nothing bled, nothing hurt. Dair touched my raised left hand with his own.

"You've healed yourself as well," Maeve said gently, coming to my side. She could talk after all, it seemed. It was all a bit too much for me. White fire flashed before my eyes again, and I fainted.

Chapter Six

The fern flower did not wilt. It continued to bloom where it lay on the grass; if anything, it grew larger and more lovely. I know, for I sat and watched it for days, lazing about and picking up twigs and things with my left hand for the sheer joy of it, stretching the arm and flexing the fingers. Hand and arm were as able as they had ever been. And Dair was as strong and well as he had ever been. I was very weak, but that was to be expected and it would pass. Dair and Maeve fussed over me enormously. I liked that, but best of all I liked it when they sat with me and talked. We talked for hours every day. None of us could get enough of it.

I was halfway to somewhere else, Dair said. *It was as if I were flying overhead, circling the World Tree and looking down on my body lying beneath it. You picked me up, and I could not feel the embrace, but I saw the—tears on your face. . . .*

That reminded me of Tirell so strongly that I almost wept again. All my anger against him was gone. I felt that I understood him now. Truth is a fearsome thing, and he had faced it in the end, as I had.

Then the sun scorched me suddenly and drove me back, Dair said.

I looked at him curiously. "Was it hard to fly?"

No! It is lovely. Well, you know I have done it before. He laughed, a blithe, barking sound. *Odd—I had so much trouble standing on my own two human feet, but none at all taking wing. I think the seasickness cured me of all such ailments at once.*

I looked up at the World Tree and the misty sky beyond,

150

wondering if I would ever be able to fly with such ease. "We all pay one way or another," I muttered.

Yes. Dair inched closer. *Frain, this brother Tirell of yours—*

Now, how had he known I was thinking of Tirell? "He paid," I said.

Yes. So did Trevyn. He smiled in that eerie, wolfish way of his. I no longer minded it.

"They are very much alike."

Yes. I have heard that Trevyn was a proper headstrong young fool—

"He certainly was!" Maeve broke in, hearing the name. She came over to us from where she had been peeling fruit nearby. "I think Trevyn and Tirell are twins of a sort, or reflections. Light and dark—Isle and Vale are both magical. Bright or black, magic is yet magic." She handed me a piece of fruit and frowned. "Frain, get something on your feet. You'll catch cold, worn out as you are." She went and fetched Dair's discarded shirt and came at me with it.

"Maeve," I said in mild annoyance, "I am all right. Why must you always be mothering me?"

She put the confounded rag on my feet and looked me full in the face. "With me it is a choice between mothering and coupling," she said.

"Oh." I swallowed. "Well, mother me as much as you like."

Sometime early in my convalescence the griffin came bounding into the meadow on its lion legs, talons upraised, stunning in the light, so golden. I thought it had come to punish me for the sake of the green things I had attacked. I knew I would not resist it, so I did not move as it ran up to me. Nor did Dair, who sat beside me.

"I am sorry," I told the griffin. "I have given my apology to all of them, and my word. It will not happen again."

To my astonishment the griffin arched its leonine body and touched its great beak to the earth at my feet. *My lord,* it said, *your pardon. You have come at last, and I did not recognize you.*

"I am no lord," I said.

Ah, but you are. Lonn D'Aeric. . . .

It was my name in the Old Language, meaning Swan Lord; I knew that by now. Elfin name or true-name, Dair called it. He had a true-name as well, but it was just his own—Dair. Everything about him was true.

151

I am greatly honored and relieved, the griffin said, still gracefully bowing. *I thought I had let in a destroyer, and all has come to good nevertheless. My lord, am I free to go?*

"I am no lord," I said.

Anyone can see that you are the greatest of lords. Please, good Lonn D'Aeric, my dismissal. . . .

"Certainly," I said dazedly. "Go."

It arose, wheeled and bounded off, let out one metallic cry and vanished into the forest. I turned to Dair.

"I am no lord," I half pleaded. But he only grinned at me in that aggravating way of his.

I let the matter drift out of my mind. I was not ready to deal with this lordship, whatever it was. For several days I lay in abeyance, letting the future take vague form in my dreams. I would return to Vale, I thought. I would be able to face Tirell now, maybe even bring about some sort of accord between him and Shamarra. Perhaps Dair and Maeve would come with me; I hated to think of parting from them. . . . I began to walk, to exercise myself, and I found that I could venture a little farther each day.

One morning I noticed that the fern flower's exquisite petals were bent far back, that they were turning fawn brown at the edges.

"You are dying!" I exclaimed. "But why?"

I AM NOT DYING IN THE USUAL CUT-FLOWER WAY, it said primly. I AM PREPARING SEED.

I remembered something about seed. "How is it to be spread?" I asked. "The wind?"

YOU WILL TAKE IT, I SUPPOSE. YOU ARE MY LORD. The fern flower droned happily to itself, a honey-humming sound. MY SCIONS WILL FLOWER THROUGHOUT THE WORLD, CONFER THE POWER. . . .

I turned away lest I say something impolite. I was getting tired of this "lord" business, and I did not want to spend the rest of my immortal life plodding about planting seeds.

SONG OF THE ONE WILL SOUND ONCE MORE.

Seedsong be damned. I had been wandering for years; I very much wanted to go back to my homeland and stay there. A lord, indeed! I was Alys's fool, as always, unless I was Shamarra's. I caught sight of a hootoo bird and kicked at a clod of lush grass before I could stop myself.

Lonn D'Aeric, said a familiar voice, THERE IS NO NEED TO SULK.

I spun about in startled recognition. It was the leafy vastness above me, the World Tree, I knew that. But the voice, aloof and amused and tender all at once. . . .

"Alys?" I cried.

"So, you know me these days." She sounded almost friendly. "I am here, as I am everywhere. I have always been within compass of your call, Frain. Can you see that now?"

"Yes," I whispered.

"Do not be so afraid. You have done well, splendidly well. I would be honored even to have you banging at me with rocks again."

I blushed and said nothing. Dair and Maeve came up to stand beside me.

"You have earned your wings, Lonn D'Aeric, Swan Lord," said Alys. "Let wings take you wherever you wish to go, with my blessing. Your quest is done."

"But—" I stopped, mired in ignorance.

"What is it?"

"The fern flower said—"

"You have done your part." She sounded amused again. "The task of spreading the seed belongs to the wandering wolf here."

He was a man at the moment. *Me?* he said, rather stupidly.

"Yes, indeed, Dair. Have you forgotten already? Are you not Trevyn's son? He brought the magic back to Isle, and you shall bring a better magic back to the mainland world, an understanding for all people, not just a special few. You have been a part of the One's greatest dream, you three travelers. Maeve understands these things when she is thinking, but you two—" Alys began to sound annoyed. "Frain, will you consider only that insignificant Vale? And Dair! You know you have been born for something special. Will you never give a thought to anything except your friend here and your next meal?"

I stole a glance at him. The look on his face was tragic.

"Oh, come, now." Alys's tone softened. "You do well enough, Dair. You are a creature of instinct, wolfwit, I know that."

Am I no longer to follow Frain at all? Dair whispered, stricken. I reached over and put an arm around him; I had to. There was a long silence.

"You may follow him yet a little while," the goddess said at last. "You will know when the time comes to leave him."

"And I am done?" I asked.

"Yes. Fly away, Frain."

"And Maeve?"

"She knows her destiny as well as I do. Ask her." The tone was one of dismissal. Golden leaves rustled as if with the passing of a spirit, then were still.

"Goodbye, Mother," Maeve murmured. "For now."

I looked at her. Though she seemed very old to me—as she had looked old ever since she had confronted Alys for my sake—in that moment she did not seem old in the dying way. Maeve reminded me of the fern flower. She seemed pregnant with something, full.

"One final form for me," she said in answer to my glance. She smiled in that gentle way of hers. "My quest is over, Frain. I will remain here, and my life will end here. Not everyone is so fortunate, to come back to their Source for life's completion."

"Are you thinking of going up as a dragonfly, perhaps?" I asked, trying to match her soft, unimpassioned tone.

"No, I am not to fly, Frain. You are the flyer. Will you soon be ready?"

I looked away to the western distance, to where the dark green treetop canopy turned bluish and met the mist. "A few days, I think."

"When you are ready, I will show you."

I walked and ate and slept and dreamed. Wings flickered in my dreams. The fern flower turned limp and entirely brown, a nut-brown seedpod growing amidst the withered petals. Then the petals fell away. The pod was firm and full. One day I felt the strength and urgency that told me it was time to fly. I went to Maeve. She looked at me and nodded, then handed the seedpod to Dair.

"It will never be depleted," she said. "It will last you till world's end." Then in a quite different tone she added, "Son, let me kiss you—".

Dair did not know how to kiss. He let her kiss him, and he nuzzled her wordlessly.

"Now. . . ." said Maeve, and she closed her eyes.

She did it so well, so beautifully. Her hair turned to feathers the color of polished bronze; they lapped around her neck like a warrior's mail, and a fringe of mane grew below. Her face was that of an eagle, with a great ivory beak; her hands were gleaming talons. With intense clarity

I noticed the amber tufts of feathers just above them, floating airily, the feathery tuft of hair at the end of her leonine tail. She was all colors of gold, shining sungold and burnished bronze; she was a griffin, and she settled in her place at the roots of the Tree, its guardian.

People will come here from time to time now, she said, *but only seers and healers may approach the Tree.*

"But the other one," I stammered, meaning the griffin in the passageway.

He is long gone. You gave him his freedom, Lonn D'Aeric. I could hear her amusement. *As was his due*, she added.

"But—" I stopped. I wanted no more of this "lord" business, and no teasing either.

You are a swan lord, she said gently. *An immortal. Fly away, Frain.*

"Farewell, Maeve," I whispered.

Farewell. Dair—tend him well.

You know I always do, Dair growled.

I faced the west, blinking, and let my thoughts take wing within me. To fly, to soar over that sea of forest, over the white mountain wall and away—somewhere out there, beyond, lay Vale—

I felt my body bend, my arms extend and russet feathers grow, flowerlike but far faster, petals tilted to the wind. No pain, but it was hard not to panic at the strangeness, even so—I had to call on an inner strength to let the change happen, as I would to let healing happen. This was much like healing in a way. I felt my vision sharpen, my body turn hard, immense muscles encasing my chest, taut pinions—I was a red hawk, and I felt all the keen windlust of the raptor.

A gray falcon stood beside me, the fern stalk held in his beak.

GIVE YOURSELF TO THE SKY, Dair said.

I gave myself to the sky as I had to desert and lake and sea. Ai, the feel of air through feathers, the whistling sound. . . . We flew. Once around the World Tree we circled—at last I could see the leaves; they were translucent jewels, aureate but oval of shape and pointed, like the gibbous moon, sun and moon in one. We did not dare aspire to the top of it—some things should remain forever hidden. We circled once and spiraled upward, red hawk and gray falcon, and then away, through the mist, and left the Source behind us.

INTERLUDE III
from The Book of Suns

Now you have known frightened men to say that the final days will come in wrath and a rain of fire and a dark abyss and the tramplings of fierce horses. But I tell you, dear children, that shame speaks in those words, and there is no need of shame and fear within the working of the pattern to its fullness. I tell you that the days of strife are now, and they will end in the sweet scent of flowers and a great peace passing into eternity and the tide of time quieting into deep ocean with scarcely a ripple. And some of you may yet live to see those days, People of Peace, and surely your descendants will.

How will it happen, that the unicorn days will come again and the song be sung once more? All that is necessary is that the magic should come back from the reaches, that the fern seed should be spread. When that passing comes the world will be filled with brightness and singing and understanding, mindful and heartfelt—birds, bears, men and wolves and quail and celandine, wind and sea, whatever is, they all will speak and understand. And no creature will need to kill or eat anymore, even so much as grass, and whatever gives of itself will do so willingly. When the panther and the deer lie down together on the heather, the heather will rejoice. And then that rejoicing will fill me and I will sing.

And then the unicorn will stand on the shore of Elwestrand. I will sing the song of the unicorn, the fair white shy one of shining horn, and when he lifts his forefoot and strikes it to that shore all the mountains of earth will dissolve and slide into the sea, softly, gently, with sunset cloud and rainbow spray, and all who watch that union will smile. And then I will sing the second song of the unicorn, and the unicorn will stand on the soft hills of Isle, and when he touches his horn to those hills the sky will come down and embrace the sea-washed earth. And I will sing the final song of the unicorn, and the white winged unicorn will spring up and fly above the land of Vale, and sun will wed with moon in a blaze of love. And day and night will once again be One, and seasons, and elements, and life and death; all who lived in the sunlit lands will be at One with unity and the infinite. And the spinning of time will stop, and the great wheel will no longer turn, the stars will swim at will in the sea and the shuttle lie still on the loom. And the pattern will be done.

What is the sign? When the Swan Lord comes to the Source and plucks the fern flower that is water and fire, those days will be on the horizon of time. And when the scion of Isle has spread the seed, those days will be at hand.

Now I have told you the tales of the Sun Kings of Isle. But who is this Swan Lord, you ask me, that we should await him? Elder Folk, he will be one who has suffered much and has earned his rest, this most blessed and consummate rest.

DAIR
REPRISE

I am Dair, who flew to Vale with Frain, side by side, wingtip to wingtip—I remember the silent bond between us. I wanted that time to last, but it went quickly. The passage did not take long, flying—only a few days. We scarcely stopped even to eat or rest. The trees did not appeal to us. They looked tiny, puny, stunted to us, and their leaves were that dull, unmagical green. In Vale the land looked bright as blood but wounded. There were great ruts and scarrings where armies had been. Summer is the season of war.

I am too late, said Frain, dismayed.

THE GODDESS SAID YOU ARE NO PART OF THIS PATTERN, I told him, mindspeaking. I could not talk even in my wolfish manner with the fern stalk clutched in my beak. WHAT WOULD YOU HAVE BEEN ABLE TO DO? I asked.

I—don't know. I just always hoped—something. To help Tirell somehow, and Shamarra.

TIRELL IS VERY KING. PERHAPS HE HAS BEEN ABLE TO HELP HIMSELF. PERHAPS HE IS ALL RIGHT.

I knew better. There was justice to be attended to. I knew that. Frain said nothing.

We followed the marks, skimming above the red soil of Vale. They led us to the court city of Melior, Frain's childhood home, all awash in water, the river gone mad, but it was still standing, shining and beautiful—Tirell must have had strong magic of his own. Frain could not speak, I could tell; his breastfeathers quivered with the force of his heartbeat. I have never fully understood childhood, myself, though I know it is a strong tug in humans. . . .

Melior was a fair place. There were young fruit trees in the courtyard, all in bloom, though their time was long past. An owl flew from the topmost tower, abroad in daylight, in strong sunlight, even.

Auguries, said Frain tightly.

There were few folk about. Tirell must have met Raz's invading army on the other side of the flooded river, and it seemed he had managed to push it back. Back, back, the trail of torn earth led, over the great central plain of Vale. We followed, and in a few moments we sighted tumult of battle on the horizon, a mass of struggling men, and those ugly Luoni swarming around it like flies around an ulcer. We dove through them—

Tirell! Frain cried. He darted downward.

I admit I had never believed all of what Frain had said about Tirell. But I believed it then, with my first look at him. I caught my breath in awe at the very sight of him. He was half a head taller than any man I had ever seen, regal and fearsome, with raven black hair and flashing eyes, godlike in beauty—it must have been hard, very hard, for Frain to have stood all those years in his shadow. Enemies swarmed about him on all sides, trying to pull him down, and he was fighting them all off, fighting like ten men, lithe and furious as a great cat. Even so, I did not see how he could prevail. And as they dragged at his arms a bald and leering king confronted him, bronze sword raised—

Frain stooped with a hawk's scream, raking the man across the shoulders with sharp talons, startling him so that he threw up his shield arm. The next moment he lost his life to Tirell's blow. Frain took human form and stood beside his brother.

"So much for Sethym," he remarked.

He spoke in the language of Vale, and I understood him. Could it be that I understood all such tongues now since the fern flower, all things? I in wolf form—I stood four-footed beside Frain, snarling, and the attackers who had hounded Tirell fell back for a moment, unnerved by my unaccountable appearance or Frain's. Tirell did not notice me. He was standing like a shaft of marble, motionless, his fair, pale face gone white as stone.

"Frain!" he gasped, sudden tears starting down his cheeks. "But how—flying in—are you a spirit?"

161

"Touch me and see," Frain invited, grinning even as the tears started from his own eyes.

In an instant they had joined in a tight embrace, hugging and pummeling each other, laughing and sobbing. I don't think they could have stayed away from each other, and such a gesture seemed to suit them, their history, that they should embrace in the midst of a battlefield. Already enemies approached them. I menaced, sending some back a step, and Frain broke away from his brother and parried a blow that had been aimed at Tirell's shoulder, picking up a dead man's dropped sword.

"Confound it, brother, don't expect me to do everything for you!" he shouted gaily, still laughing through tears. "Defend yourself! There is a row going on here."

Tirell cleared a space around himself with a single mighty swipe of his long blade. But the press of battle was hard, and a struggling, trampling mass of men came between him and Frain. And then Frain started fighting in earnest.

I had heard once of a long-ago folk who had done battle naked, without even helms, hair flying free, glorying in the strength and skill of their exposed bodies, with only a bare sword for protection—Frain fought that way, magnificent. Amidst all the shining bronze he gleamed splendid with his own sheen, sweat sheen—or was it something more, glow of power? Wholeness, unity of self and purpose had given him great power, unicorn power. He could do nothing wrong, no harm could come to him, his sword moved as if guided by magic, faultlessly, faster than the eye could follow, as he opened a way for himself, cut a path straight as the unicorn's horn through the clash of armies to his brother's side, and I followed in his wake, skulking.

Tirell had taken a cut on the forehead. But those who attacked him dropped back as we drew near, and he paused a moment in his labors of war to look at us.

"Like a god," he marveled softly. "Mighty shoulders and two strong arms. . . . What is that furry thing sheltering at your feet?"

"A friend." Frain turned to stand at Tirell's side. "Come on, brother," he invited, his tone fierce and joyous. "We will take them together."

They touched hands briefly in warbond.

"Where's that Raz?"

162

"Up ahead," Tirell said.

We formed line of battle, the three of us. Tirell roared at his men to follow and we pressed forward, Frain flanking Tirell to the left and I to the right, bristling hugely and hoping no warrior would come near me, for this sort of combat was new and strange and terrible to me, all smiting and cries and straining legs, far too many and too much— I might have been killed several times over, but I walked under the protection of Tirell's long sword. He fought splendidly, and Frain with all the golden force of his lordship, and they overcame or overawed all whom they met, True King and Swan Lord. We made our way steadily forward.

"There, a bit left," Tirell said grimly at last. "By the snakes."

My hackle hairs rose unbidden. Great serpents reared their vicious, flat and pointed heads above the battlefield, each one twice the height of a man. In their midst, and flanked by a bodyguard of bronze-helmed footsoldiers as well, rode Raz the renegade canton king. His mount stood seventeen hands and massive, giving him a borrowed stature—he had none of his own. Even at the distance, all gilded and jeweled and lapped in armor and wrapped in fine robes, he showed for what he was—short, fat, and, by his posture, arrogant.

"I am not looking forward to taking on the snakes," Tirell added. "I have heard that they spit."

Venom, he meant. I tried not to cringe.

"No need," said Frain. "Let us just make a little space here."

Tirell set to work without hesitation, clearing away enemies, and Frain stood still, gazing ahead intently toward where the serpents loomed.

"*Laifrita thae, arledas!*" he called, a high, carrying shout that sped the distance as if on wings. "Sweet peace to thee, earth-brothers!" It was the creature tongue I knew from my earliest days and loved, the Old Language. Just hearing it, I felt blessed.

"Primal folk, leave that worthless king and go back to your own ways. The mountain caverns are calling to you, earthcreepers!"

Of one accord the great heads of the snakes swiveled around to look at him, while Raz also stared, startled.

Who speaks? one serpent challenged.

"I, Lonn D'Aeric. I bid you go."

The serpents turned and slid away. Frain spoke again, and the steed that bore Raz sprang forward through the ranks of his startled guards. It carried him up to us in spite of all his shouting and sawing at the reins, and Tirell's army cheered and surged forward, surrounding us. Tirell reached up and pulled the stout king off. He fell with a thump on the ground. Raz was no fighter—he never even drew the sword he wore.

"Mercy, my liege king," he begged, his voice oily even in his despair.

I glanced at Tirell and saw that he was not without thoughts of mercy. Bellflower blue shadow in his eyes showed that. Then they hardened to the color of blue ice—he was True King, and a king who allows revolt is no king.

"I have a wife," he told Raz almost quietly, "the most loving and faithful of wives, your daughter, and you tried to lure her away from me by the most vile slanders. And when that failed, you sent ruffians to steal our son. Now at last you have found nerve to make open battle on me. No, Raz. I have no mercy to offer you."

"Mer—" the man started again, but before he could finish his head was gone. A more vindictive monarch would have killed him at greater length, but Tirell made the slaying swift. A roar of victory went up from his army as they hoisted the head on a spear for proof, and a groan from the others. Losing heart, they started to fall back, and Tirell's followers cheered, pressing after. Tirell stood still, leaning on his sword, looking tired and more than a little sickened, letting the battle leave him.

"It is over," he murmured.

"Not yet, brother." Frain looked tired as well, but keen of glance. "You have not yet met your real enemy."

"Myself?" Tirell straightened, smiling broadly. "I thought I had."

"Son of Aftalun, Tirell, I know you have!" Frain sounded both amused and annoyed. "I mean Shamarra."

"She. Shamarra." Tirell's smile faded, and the same keen look came into his eyes. "For years I feared her, until I came to believe she had left Vale for good."

"She is here. She is a shape changer, so she could be anything, anywhere. A beetle in the earth, one of those Luoni—" Frain lifted his sword briefly toward the ugly

164

birdwomen who swooped overhead. "Even that horse, I thought, until it obeyed me."

"Shamarra," Tirell breathed. "She whom I wronged. I should have known——" He lifted his sword, taking the wary stance of a warrior. "What is going on now?"

The sun was going dark. All in a moment it seemed to be blotted out in the midst of the cloudless sky. The clash of weapons abruptly stopped.

"Men of Melior to me!" Tirell shouted.

Either they did not hear him or they were too stricken to obey. Warriors of both armies started scattering and straggling in all directions, running, terrified of the unnatural dusk. The battle lines faded away until only a great heap and strewing of bodies remained. The day seemed much too quiet then, horribly so, with no sound except for the groaning of wounded men and the greedy squawks of the Luoni. Frain and Tirell stood alone on the bloodied plain with a whining wolf, myself.

"What is it?" Frain asked softly, expecting no reply. For my own part I was crouching and bristling in fear. Then a streak of fire shot through the gloom, and I understood. More portents. Comets fly when great men die.

"Surely this pother cannot be all for Raz," said Tirell uncertainly.

"There," Frain whispered, pointing his blade.

A stirring amid a pile of corpses, stench, glimmer of fungus-white flesh, a sluggish heave and we saw it—a monstrous maggot, as daunting as death, its stubby tip standing man-high and wriggling hideously. But there was not time to stare or flee, it had taken a greenish change, it was a serpent as vast as the others and more fearsome, for just at its neck sprouted feathered wings.

"Ai!" Frain shouted, an incoherent cry of alarm, and it flew at us.

"The black beast," Tirell said, very low.

I do not know what he meant by that. But in the moment he spoke the thing was indeed a beast, an unnatural creature made all of flux, the pale deathly deer, horned catamount fleet as a deer, goblin horse, snarling antlered hound of hell. Like a whirlwind it sped toward us, all a blur of fear and confusion, and Tirell stood rock steady, waiting for it. But Frain sprang forward and ran to meet it.

"Shamarra, no!" he shouted. "You shall not have him!"

She veered to slip past him, but he blocked her way swiftly with his sword, and she came to a halt just before him, shimmering eerily from one form to the next.

And who are you to say I must not have my game, Swan Lord? she asked. The cool voice was familiar, yet with none of the former condescension in it. *I thought you loved me,* she added, and there was something of real feeling in the words despite her horrifying formless form.

"I do! You know I am fated to do so. But I love my brother as well, and for more reason. Am I to let one of you slay the other, then?" Frain raised his sword in threat as, a horned and ram-headed serpent, she oozed forward.

You will not kill me.

"Perhaps not. But I am your equal now; beware."

Very true. Was that warmth in her voice, congratulation, even? *Perhaps more than my equal at most times. But just now the sun is in abeyance, Lonn D'Aeric, and for that reason I think you will not be able to stand against me.*

An odd, inquiring look washed over Frain's face. "Not your doing, surely?" he murmured.

No. Wry humor in Shamarra's voice—they understood each other, these two! *No, scarcely. Sun says that yon king's death is in the pattern, Frain. I seek justice, no more. Now let me pass.*

He stood his ground. "We must make a new pattern," he declared, or begged. "One of forgiveness, reconciliation—"

"Only one way is that possible," said a strong and quiet voice.

It was Tirell who spoke. He had understood all that was said—he must truly have been one who had learned from dragons. He stepped forward a pace, sword raised.

"You know well enough how such healing comes, Frain," he said. "I must face the thing I fear. Is it not so?"

A strange sort of thunder sounded, earthly thunder, and beneath our feet the ground shook. Frain swayed where he stood.

"Tirell—I cannot let it happen!" he cried. But he had turned slightly to the sound of his brother's voice, and the nameless creature that was Shamarra swept past him, gave a mighty leap and was on us.

I say us because I still stood at Tirell's side. I sprang to a deathgrip on the shapeshifting thing's throat, and Tirell's sword met its chest, plunged deep. But the creature surged

166

forward, as fluid as water, taking me with it like a leaf. It ran right up Tirell's sword and sank the many tines of its antlers into his chest, raped him with them tenfold, drove its way into him—and then with a mighty toss of its head it threw me off and ripped him open. Then it staggered away and fell. It lay dying, and it was the fair and maidenly Shamarra who lay there, a sword buried to the hilt in her bosom.

The Luoni flapped down and sat in a nearby copse, waiting.

Tirell lay—I could not look at him, I could not look anywhere. His chest was torn out, and his burning blue eyes gazed up at the darkened sun, frosted over with pain. Frain stood for a moment as stunned as I, staring at his brother, staring at Shamarra. Then he went to Tirell without speaking, laid gentle hands on his forehead and heaving sides. He lifted the prone head, sat and cradled it in his arms. Tears were running silently down his cheeks.

"And a healer, yet," Tirell marveled. His pain had left him at that touch. He spoke readily and lay in merciful ease. But Frain could scarcely speak for anguish.

"This is all the help I can offer you," he said in a choked voice. There was no mighty Tree in that place. He could not save his brother from death as he had saved me.

"You have brought me your forgiveness," said Tirell faintly. "That is the greatest of help and healing." He let his head rest against Frain's chest, and for a moment he closed his jewel-bright eyes. Frain stifled a sob.

"With all my heart," he averred.

"And perhaps even Shamarra's. . . ."

Shamarra lay nearby, quite still and senseless, breathing only in shallow gasps.

"She has hurt herself as much as me," Tirell murmured. "Frain. . . ." The word was an entreaty and a caress.

"What?" Frain whispered.

"The Luoni will attack me. I am many times forsworn."

Frain touched his temples. "We will fly with you and protect you, my friend and I," he promised. He laid his face close to the bloodless one he held. "I love you, brother," he said.

Shamarra went up as a swan, a fair white swan, the proper form of the immortal. I saw it go—perhaps things were manifest to me by then that would have been unseen before. Tirell went up as an eagle, the great black-and-white ger-eagle, at nearly the same moment, and Frain and I sprang up to be after him. Red hawk and gray falcon, we were beside him in a flash, and the Luoni swooped down on all of us, screeching.

Laifrita thae, earthsisters, Frain told them. *Give us passage.*

Laifrita thae, deadly ones, I greeted them courteously.

They could not attack us who lived and tendered them the greeting. They wanted Tirell badly, but Frain and I flew to either side of him and Shamarra just above, the swan lady protecting her detested lover, and sharp talons curved below. The Luoni flapped about us, cursing.

Shamarra? Tirell asked.

It is all gone. She sounded glad. *All hatred purged with the passing. I only remember that you were fair.*

I thank you, Lady, he said.

Short, swift and wild that flight was, but it was glorious. The way led to the west, where the great river ran, a broad, bright flow. Just as we came over it the sun burst forth from its bonds of darkness, far down the western sky, and touched everything with sudden gold. Tirell saluted his brother and made his whistling dive, disappeared into the shining water on his way to Aftalun's realm. The Luoni wheeled away, complaining, and Shamarra sailed onward, majestic, into the sunset. She would fly with the immortal flocks. . . . On the instant Frain shot after her.

No wait! I cried. *I have to go back*—I had left the fern seed behind. And already I had forgotten that his quest was different from mine. *Frain, farewell!* I called out, my voice cracking, and I turned back to where Tirell's body lay, my heart half breaking. When I reached the battle place I found my fern seed easily enough, but the sight of that fair young True King, dead, turned me human in form, mirrored my own grief. I sat down and wept. When Frain came, only a few minutes behind me, I could not stop weeping.

He put his arms around me even as the feathers were leaving them. "I must part from you soon," he said gently. "A few more days. There is something I must do."

What is it? I asked, still sobbing.

"You will see. Shamarra has told me what I must do."

I looked at him, calming myself with an effort, sniffling. Tracks of tears were on his face, but he seemed too tired to sorrow anymore.

168

Does she no longer despise you, then? I asked.

"I think not. All such spleen seems gone from her."

I doubted him. But then, I had doubted him about Tirell.

"Look, the light is fading," Frain said. "We will have to stay here tonight."

We were both exhausted and heartsore, too spent even to properly sleep. Scent of blood was on the air, and wails of women come to collect their dead and dying. We dozed restlessly and woke often with little cries in the night and spoke to each other for comfort. Dawn, at last—we got up and smoothed Tirell's cold brow, closed his bright blue eyes. There were no rocks to build a cairn for him—

Moved by some new instinct, I got the fern seed pod, carefully opened the pointed end of it and shook out a mist of seed so fine it could scarcely be seen. Then I stood openmouthed, joy growing in me and bursting into bloom. For the ferns sprang up even as I watched, unfurling bright plumes of green, surrounding Tirell with their soft stirring, raising their canopy over him, and each one of them held up a flower of fire red with petals that seemed to float on air.

"You've made a memorial for him," Frain breathed. "Dair, you marvel—"

Hush, I grumped. *Can we go now?*

"Yes. In fact, we must."

We walked off westward. Neither of us felt like flying just then, but human walking is a wearisome business. *Can you be a wolf?* I asked Frain, going wolf myself.

He thought about it, and then he made the change. But instead of a wolf it was a wolflike dog that stood beside me—red, of course, with silky fur, finer than mine, and sensitive petal-like ears. He was a staghound, emblem of honor and fidelity.

I should have known, I said.

Wolf and dog. He grinned at me toothily. *Come on.*

We trotted along companionably, covering the miles without much effort. I could not hunt, for I held the fern stalk in my mouth. But we met a peasant woman who, oddly, did not seem afraid of us, and she gave us food. We swam the river and crossed the farms and fields of Melior. We met the peasant woman again the second day, she with her apron full of bread and meat, and I could not

169

help but look at her askance, for how could she be there ahead of us?

Mother of us all, said Frain softly, *you are good to us. Thank you.*

"One more day and you will be each on his own," she said. "Eat well."

We ate and slept and went on. The steep, dark mountains of Acheron loomed before us. We trotted into a forest of gray and twisted trees. Some of them looked half dead, but they might have been two hundred years old and ready for two hundred more. The trees of Acheron are deceptive things, like its water. They stooped over the trail like so many old women, and we could hear them talking.

So the lady has flown at last, one creaked.

That is what the small birds say, tittered another in tones of doubt. They were gossips.

If it is true, the Swan Lord should come soon, rustled a third.

Do we get to set root in Melior at last? the first one asked. We could level the castle stock and stone.

I doubt it, they said. When I see I'll believe. They joined in a dry, whispering chorus. What matter, what matter the dooms men foretell! Lords and ladies come and go, and it is all the same to us. Death goes on dying, and we stand behind the wall.

They were wrong.

What is this? one said with a sigh of limp leaves. A wolf and a dog, side by side?

We broke into a lope and left them behind. Steep slopes of loose rock met us, then sheer crags. But we went surely on our clever paws, and Frain knew the way, for he had been here twice before. The peasant woman met us and fed us once more on toward evening, and then we slept and made the final journey to the lake.

The lake where it had all begun for Frain, the lake I had once seen on an old woman's loom. Set so much as a foot in the water, folk said, and your own darkness would drag you down. If not, you would become immortal, but eternally in thrall to whatever passions touched you at the time. . . . It was a deathly lake. High up amid the mountain peaks it lay, in a dark and secluded valley, the water very dim and very still. Far out in the middle of the mirrorlike expanse floated a single swan, a black swan, its left wing trailing in the water, crippled. The image in the water below it was white. Along the far verge, beneath some willow trees, lay a white winged unicorn. Its reflection in the glimmering water was black.

"This is the most perilous of places, the most dangerous of lakes, Dair," Frain told me softly. "Don't go near the water or look into it, or I can't say what might happen to you."

He had taken his human form, and I took my own at the sight of him. And he went to the water's edge, as he had told me not to. He knelt there and looked so long that I wondered if he might be bewitched. Slowly, uncertainly, I walked up behind him. There were odd four-petaled flowers at the grassy verge, white, and black flowers floated in the shallows below them, or so it seemed. Frain's freckled face looked up from among them—just his own face, reflected, nothing more. Puzzled, I glanced toward where my own shadow lay. But Frain, suddenly aware of me, jumped up with a shout and lunged at me, wrestling me away with both arms.

"Dair!" he exclaimed anxiously. "Did you see—"

Nothing but myself. Only my own peculiar face had looked back at me from the shadowshining water. Frain let go of me with a huge sigh.

"I should have known," he muttered. "You are as pure as I was. Dair, what a fright you gave me! I told you—"

What did you see? I asked, to head him off. I wanted no quarrel. Not this last day.

"Myself. Somewhat darkly, but nothing too terribly hard to bear." He looked out at the middle of the lake. "There is my swan," he said. "Well . . ." He turned back to me for a moment, laying his hand on my shoulder. "Dair, goodbye."

Fear clenched me. *Frain, wait,* I begged. *I don't understand. What are you going to do?*

"Give myself to the lake."

But why? I tried to contain my horror. The white moonmark, sign of the kiss of the All-Mother, shone faintly on his cheek, and there was a sureness about him.

"You have your task." His hand gentled my arm as he patiently explained. "And I need my rest. . . . Dair, I love her still, I always will, it is fated on me, but the love is a torment in me because in this body I hate her as well. I am

171

tired, too much has happened and I remember it all too well, I bear scars. She has gone beyond that now, and if I do the same—if I take a different form from which I may not return, why—there is a chance. . . ."

He looked away over the towering mountains that made a barrier to the west.

"I know it will seem odd, Dair, but—it is the only way for me. Truly. And it will be—healing of an innocent thing."

The swan swam a little closer, trailing its crippled wing.

"Goodbye," Frain muttered, and he hugged me, hard. I felt his face against my own and I felt tears—my own. He turned away. I stopped him with a touch, but he would not face me again, only half turned toward me.

"Dair, I have to go!" The words were choked. Tears on his face, too.

I know. Frain, if you should ever see Trevyn—in this world or another—

He looked at me then, eager, smiling. "I will go to him straightway. What would you like me to tell him?"

Just say that—I am well.

"I'll tell him far more than that."

He embraced me once more, touched my hand. Then he turned and, with scarcely a ripple, waded into the lake.

It did not take him. I could see quite clearly that it had no power over him at all. He waded in until the water was up to his head and the swan swam a little way ahead of him, and then he gave himself to the lake, he disappeared. I watched for long moments, scarcely daring to blink, sure I would see him again but frightened for him as well—

And the water reached up, the white reflection in the lake reached up and embraced the swan, and the swan lifted its wings with a shout of exultation, crippled no longer. It was black no longer, either, it was white, sea-foam white, lotuspetal white, with a sort of golden sheen about it, an aureole, and it took wing, it soared. It sang— I had never known Frain to sing, but I knew it was he, even so, and the song was one of victory and joy. Triumph, triumph, swan, windmaster, winging, singing through the sky. . . . The swan flew once over my head, calling a clear greeting, and then it lifted like thistleseed over the westward mountains, sang yet again and was gone. Watching, I found that I was weeping and singing aloud for love and loneliness—howling, if you will. I was a wolf, after all.

172

Laifrita thae, Frain. Sweet peace to thee. Fly away.

I padded off through the mountains with the fern seed held in my mouth. I passed out of Vale into the lands beyond and planted seed when the mood took me. Sometimes I dreamed of Frain or of Trevyn, and the dreams comforted me.

Epilogue

On a golden day when summer was thinking of autumn, King Trevyn of Isle rode homeward toward Laueroc from Rodsen. As he rode a great white swan whistled overhead, a swan with an aureate glow that reminded him of certain unaccountable legends he had lately heard, the most splendid of swans. Seeing him, it circled back. *Alberic*, it greeted him by his elfin name.

"Lonn D'Aeric," said Trevyn with a wondering smile. "Swan Lord." He got down from his horse to meet an equal, and the creature landed in the grass beside him.

"So the final age is truly at hand," Trevyn murmured. "Peace passing into eternity—"

Dair asked me to tender you his greeting, the swan said.

"Frain!" Trevyn exclaimed.

Folk used to call me by that name. I scarcely remember. . . . The swan arched his lovely neck. *But I remember Dair. He is*—Even the Old Language would not encompass what Lonn D'Aeric felt. He bowed his graceful head in a sort of homage.

He is a marvel beyond belief, my lord.

"So you came to love him at last," said Trevyn softly.

I learned to love him, and all else followed.

"I can scarcely believe that you are really come," Trevyn said in a hushed voice. "All striving drawing to an end, yours and everyone's, soon to be done for all time. . . . What is for you now, Lonn D'Aeric?"

The wide dim sea and that western land—what is its name?

"Elwestrand."

They talked for a while longer, of Dair wandering with